EVERYMAN, I will go with thee,

and be thy guide,

In thy most need to go by thy side

SIR HUGH SEYMOUR WALPOLE

Born in New Zealand in 1884, the son of a bishop. Came to England at the age of five, and was educated at King's School, Canterbury, and Emmanuel College, Cambridge. After a short experience as a schoolmaster he settled in Chelsea, and took up literary journalism. Served with the Russian Red Cross from 1914 to 1916, and was later in charge of British propaganda at Petrograd. He was knighted in 1937 and died in 1941.

HUGH WALPOLE

Mr Perrin and Mr Traill

PREFACE BY THE AUTHOR

'The way here also was very wearisome through dirt and shabbiness: nor was there on all this ground so much as one inn or victualling-house wherein to refresh the feebler sort.'—*Pilgrim's Progress.*

DENT: LONDON
EVERYMAN'S LIBRARY

Made in Great Britain
at the
Aldine Press · Letchworth · Herts
for
J. M. DENT & SONS LTD
Aldine House · Bedford Street · London
First included in Everyman's Library 1935
Last reprinted 1961

No. 1918 ISBN: 0 460 01918 x

PREFACE

It is nearly twenty-five years since this novel was first published and it is (I suppose) quite natural that I should have a feeling of gratification at the book's liveliness after all this time. I will frankly confess that I have some irritation in regard to it, an irritation that every author feels when an early book of his is steadily preferred to later ones. A writer likes to feel that he is improving. although what really happens to any kind of artist is that he goes up and down, in and out, blindly following an impulse which is sometimes a true one, sometimes very false indeed.

Certain friends of mine, a number of critics, consider that three novels, and three only, by me deserve the name of literature—*Mr. Perrin, The Dark Forest,* and *The Old Ladies.* I mention this because all three of these books arose out of very definite actual experiences. *Mr. Perrin* and *The Dark Forest* are almost literal transcriptions of events that occurred to me, seen of course in the light of my own character and personality. *The Old Ladies* also arose out of a very real adventure: imagination did something to it, but in the main it remains true to history. It would seem, then, that literary criticism of our time and the literary personal taste of sophisticated people prefers greatly that its novelists should write realistically from actual experience. *The Way of All Flesh, The Old Wives' Tale, Of Human Bondage*—these are the novels that are praised, and rightly praised, in our time. But it has not always been so. A fairy story, a macabre dream, a spiritual history—all these things, very unpopular until the last year or two, will return, and the creator who relies more upon the inference behind the fact than upon the fact itself, more upon the dream than the actual business, more upon the intangible world of poetry than the actual world of concrete evidence, this kind of creator will come into his kingdom once again.

As I throw myself back through all those years and try to remember what kind of circumstances accompanied the writing of *Mr. Perrin and Mr. Traill,* I am bewildered by the tricks that memory will play. I remember very definitely certain things. *Mr. Perrin* was the third of my published novels. The year before it there had come a book, *Maradick at Forty* by name, which was a youthful attempt to put the Devil on to the Cornish coast. This was a very romantic novel indeed, for not only did it contain my idea of the Devil but also my notion of married life about which I knew nothing; and the Cornish coast was nothing like the real Cornish coast at all. It disappointed a number of people who had been interested in my first book, and I was scolded considerably. Nevertheless, I began a third romantic novel which had the odd title of *The Crabtree.* I had written some eight chapters of this and was in a pretty considerable muddle. I remember nothing about it at all except that its background was contemporary Chelsea. I was walking one afternoon towards Sloane Square, where I was going to occupy a seat in the gallery of the Court Theatre, as I did regularly once a week in order to enjoy play after play of the Barker-Vedrenne management. I was in the very middle of the King's Road when I suddenly saw Mr. Perrin staring at me. By the time that I had reached the Court Theatre, a brief five minutes, the whole of the story was outlined in my mind. It sprang into reality from the Umbrella incident which had actually occurred. I remember that as I climbed the stairs to the gallery I thought of the title. The book should be called *Green Apple Orchard*—an affected title; I am happy to think that it did not last very long. When I considered the story—it was driving me relentlessly far away from the *Crabtree*—I did not realize at all that I was going to be realistic now instead of romantic. The figures in *Maradick* were every bit as real and true to me as were Mr. Perrin and Mr. Traill.

The only difference was that they were not so real to other people. It seemed to me that it was a much finer thing to write about people whom one had never met, to create them in fact in a world of one's own, than to transcribe the habits and weaknesses of people one knew. This I quite deliberately intended to do in *Mr. Perrin,* and I should like to say here and now that in the whole of my writing life it was the one and only time that I intended anything of the kind.

I think it is worth while to stop for a moment and consider this important question. Mr Somerset Maugham, who has frequently been accused of putting into his books people who are directly taken from real life, has argued very ably in several prefaces in defence of the practice, or rather he has said, what is absolutely true, that it is quite impossible for an artist to put down on paper (if he has any creative power at all) a portrait of someone he knows—the portrait will change in his hand. Quite so; but the real trouble lies in the surviving fragments of the actual person. Much is added by the creator, but enough remains for the Leigh Hunts, the Savage Landors, the Sidney Webbs, and the others to recognize themselves pretty clearly, or if they do not recognize themselves, their friends do the job for them very efficiently. *Moi qui parle*—I have suffered and I know, and I frankly consider that there has been in my time a great deal too much of this. It is inartistic, often very cruel and always unnecessary.

I can honestly say that I have never quite recovered in my own spirit from the half-portraits in *Mr. Perrin.* The facts were very simply that I had been for a year schoolmaster at Epsom College, but I had hated being a schoolmaster and escaped at the first possible moment. Epsom College is a splendid school with a grand history and has supplied for the world many of its finest doctors. When I was there the masters were undoubtedly too closely crowded in upon one another. But what was more undoubted was that I was entirely unsuited to be a schoolmaster. For one thing, my eye was constantly fixed on the possibility of running away to London and starting there a writing career. For another thing, I was sublimely ignorant of the subjects I was supposed to teach. One confession will suffice. I was French Master for some of the older forms and my French was so bad, my pronunciation of it so shocking, that I would occupy my French hour in telling my form the story in English, and this story they should afterwards translate into French. Of course if a master is inadequate for his job other masters very quickly perceive it; and a good deal of unhappiness arose from my own conscience, for I knew that I was taking money under false pretences. All these things made me a bad schoolmaster and a bad companion to other schoolmasters. I can only say now, after twenty five years, that every one treated me with a kindness and consideration that I never deserved. I repaid them by putting caricatures of most of them into this book and especially of one lady who had been always kind and generous to me. And yet, at the back of the book, there was something real. I know now that, in my immature ignorance, I struck by chance upon an element in modern life which is true of many careers besides schoolmastering. There is in this book a kind of claustrophobia and that is one of the most terrible elements of this our post-war existence.

By one of those pieces of good luck that sometimes brighten the lives of authors, I found a dramatic subject which almost any one encountering it in a book would declare to be true. Schoolmasters are not slaves, but for any one who is trying to be a schoolmaster and hates it the elements of slavery are there.

Then, of course, there, is a strain of self-pity in the book. While the young, bouyant, vital Mr. Traill was what I would have liked to be, the tortured, half-maddened Mr. Perrin was what I thought I was. As a matter of fact, of course, I was neither. I was a happy young man, who enjoyed playing football and running up to London to the theatre, but did not enjoy the consciousness that he was doing his work badly and that every one around him knew it.

Now it was exactly in this sublimation of myself—

that is in the imagined image of Mr. Perrin rather than in the photographic portraits of real people—I showed that I was a creative writer and not only a reporter. It was the realistic element in the book that made it significant, not significant in the way my friend Compton Mackenzie's *Sinister Street*, published about the same time, and D. H. Lawrence's wonderful *Sons and Lovers*, were significant. It had nothing of the size of these two books, but it was a little victory won in the same battle. About 1910 H. G. Wells gave his famous lecture at The Times' Book Club, in which he declared that we had enough of romantic nonsense and that novels must deal with real people and be afraid of nothing. All through the nineties and the early nineteen-hundreds the English novel had been persistently romantic. From Stevenson to Maurice Hewlett's fine *Queen's Quair* romantic victories had been scored all along the line. The very young novelists of 1910—Compton Mackenzie, D. H. Lawrence, Francis Brett Young, Gilbert Cannan, W. L. George, Viola Meynell, myself, and others—all felt that they must tell the truth about life, or perish in the attempt. But I personally was sure that the kind of truth I told in *Mr. Perrin* was not enough. I struggled to find something more deeply significant, more spiritually revealing, and I have been struggling to find that ever since. Nevertheless *Mr. Perrin* remains as one of the early realistic novels at the beginning of the realistic period, from 1910 to 1930.

I am proud that it has survived to find its place in *Everyman's*. I certainly never suspected all those years ago that the book would do more in the world than rouse much indignation in the breasts of the staff of Epsom College. I wanted it to do that. It did. Now I am very sorry and I hope that they have forgiven me.

H. WALPOLE.

1955.

SELECT BIBLIOGRAPHY

Dates are those of first publication in book form.

The Wooden Horse, 1909; *Maradick at Forty*, 1910; *Mr. Perrin and Mr. Traill*, 1911; *The Prelude to Adventure*, 1912; *Fortitude*, 1913; *The Duchess of Wrexe*, 1914; *The Golden Scarecrow*, 1915; *The Dark Forest*, 1916; *The Green Mirror*, 1918; *The Secret City*, 1919; *Jeremy*, 1919; *The Captives*, 1920; *The Thirteen Travellers*, 1921; *The Young Enchanted*, 1921; *The Cathedral*, 1922; *Jeremy and Hamlet*, 1923; *The Old Ladies*, 1924; *Portrait of a Man with Red Hair*, 1925; *Harmer John*, 1926; *Jeremy at Crale*, 1927; *Wintersmoon*, 1928; *The Silver Thorn*, 1928; *Hans Frost*, 1929; *Rogue Herries*, 1930; *Above the Dark Circus*, 1931; *Judith Paris*, 1931; *The Fortress*, 1932; *All Souls' Night*, 1933; *Vanessa*, 1933; *Captain Nicholas*, 1934; *The Inquisitor*, 1935; *A Prayer for My Son*, 1936; *John Cornelius*, 1937; *Head in Green Bronze*, 1938; *The Joyful Delaneys*, 1938; *The Sea Tower*, 1939; *Roman Fountain*, 1940; *The Bright Pavilions*, 1940; *The Blind Man's House*, 1941; *The Slain*, 1942; *Katherine Christian*, 1944.

Walpole also wrote a 'novel in letters,' in collaboration with J. B. Priestley, called *Farthing Hall*, 1929. His miscellaneous work consists of studies of Conrad and Trollope (1916 and 1928), *The English Novel* (Rede Lecture, 1926), a volume on *Reading* (1926), *The Apple Trees: Four Reminiscences* (1933), and a small 'affirmation,' *My Religious Experience* (1928).

In addition he wrote a play, *The Young Huntress* (1933), and two of his novels have been dramatized: *The Cathedral* (1932) and *The Old Ladies* (1935).

See also Marguerite Steen, *Hugh Walpole: a study*, 1933; R. Hart-Davis, *Hugh Walpole: a Biography*, 1952, 1963

TO

PUNCH

MY DEAR PUNCH,

There are a thousand and one reasons why I should dedicate this book to you. It would take a very long time and much good paper to give you them all; but here, at any rate, is one of them. Do you remember a summer day last year that we spent together? The place was a little French town, and we climbed its high, crooked street, and had tea in an inn at the top—an inn with a square courtyard, bad, impossible tea, and a large black cat.

It was on that afternoon that I introduced you for a little time to Mr. Perrin, and you, because you have more understanding and sympathy than any one I have ever met, understood him and sympathized. For the good things that you have done for me I can never repay you, but for the good things that you did on that afternoon for Mr. Perrin I give you this book.

Yours affectionately,

HUGH WALPOLE.

CHELSEA, *January* 1911.

CONTENTS

CHAPTER I

MR. VINCENT PERRIN DRINKS HIS TEA AND GIVES MR. TRAILL SOUND ADVICE

I

VINCENT PERRIN said to himself again and again as he climbed the hill: 'It shall be all right this term'—and then, 'It *shall* be'—and then, '*This* term.' A cold wintry sun watched him from above the brown shaggy wood on the horizon; the sky was a pale and watery blue, and on its surface white clouds edged with grey lay like saucers. A little wind sighed and struggled amongst the hedges, because Mr. Perrin had nearly reached the top of the hill, and there was always a breeze there. He stopped for a moment and looked back. The hill on which he was stood straight out from the surrounding country; it was shaped like a sugar loaf, and the red-brown earth of its fields seemed to catch the red light of the sun; behind it was green, undulating country, in front of it the blue, vast sweep of the sea.

'It *shall* be all right this term,' said Mr. Perrin, and he pulled his rather faded greatcoat about his ears, because the little wind was playing with the short bristly hairs at the back of his neck. He was long and gaunt; his face might have been considered strong had it not been for the weak chin and a shaggy, unkempt moustache of a nondescript pale brown. His hands were long and bony, and the collar that he wore was too high, and propped his neck up, so that he had the effect of someone who strained to overlook something. His eyes were pale and watery, and his eyebrows of the same sandy colour as his moustache. His age was about forty-five, and he had been a master at Moffatt's for over twenty years. His back was a little bent as he walked; his hands were folded behind his back, and he carried a rough, ugly walking-stick that trailed along the ground.

His eyes were fixed on the enormous brown block of buildings on the top of the hill in front of him: he did not see the sea, nor the sky, nor the distant Brown Wood.

The air was still with the clear suspense of an early autumn day. The sound of a distant mining stamp drove across space with the ring of a hammer, and the tiny whisper—as of someone who tells eagerly, but mysteriously, a secret—was the beating of the waves far at the bottom of the hill against the rocks.

Faint blue smoke hung against the saucer-shaped clouds above the chimneys of Moffatt's; in the air there was a sharp scented smell of some hidden bonfire.

The silence was broken by the sound of wheels, and an open cab drove up the hill. In it were seated four small boys, surrounded by a multitude of bags, hockey-sticks, and rugs. The four small boys were all very small indeed, but they sat up when they saw Mr. Perrin, and touched their hats with a simultaneous movement. Mr. Perrin nodded sternly, glanced at them for a moment, and then switched his eyes back to the brown buildings again.

'Barker Minor, French, Doggett, and Rogers,' he said to himself quickly; 'Barker Minor, French . . .'; then his mind swung back to its earlier theme again, and he said out aloud, hitting the road with his stick, 'It shall *be* all right *this* term.'

The school clock—he knew the sound so well that he often thought he heard it at home in Buckinghamshire—struck half-past three. He hastened his steps. His holidays had been good—better than usual; he had played golf well; the men at the club had not been quite such idiots and fools as they usually were: they had listened to him quite patiently about Education—shall it be Greek or German? Public School Morality, and What a Mother can do for her Boy—all favourite subjects of his.

Perhaps this term was not going to be so bad—perhaps the new man would be an acquisition: he could not, at any rate, be *worse* than Searle of the preceding term. The new man was, Perrin had heard, only just down from the University—he would probably do what Perrin suggested.

No, this term was to be all right. He never liked the autumn term; but there were a great many new boys, his house was full, and then—he stopped once more and drew a deep breath—there was Miss Desart. He tried to twist the end of his moustache, but some hairs were longer than others, and he never could obtain a combined movement.... Miss Desart.... He coughed.

He passed in through the black school gates, his shabby coat flapping at his heels.

The distant Brown Wood, as it surrendered to the sun, flamed with gold; the dark green hedges on the hill slowly caught the light.

II

The masters' common room in the Lower School was a small square room that was inclined in the summer to get very stuffy indeed. It stood, moreover, exactly between the kitchen, where meals were prepared, and the long dining-room, where meals were eaten, and there was therefore a perpetual odour of food in the air. On a 'mutton day'—there were three 'mutton' days a week—this odour hung in heavy, clammy folds about the ceiling, and on those days there were always more boys kept in than on the other days—on so small a thing may punishment hang.

To-day—this being the first day of the term—the room was exeedingly tidy. On the right wall, touching the windows, were two rows of pigeon-holes, and above each pigeon-hole was printed, on a white label, a name—'Mr. Perrin,' 'Mr. Dormer,' 'Mr. Clinton,' 'Mr. Traill.'

Each master had two pigeon-holes into which he might put his papers and his letters; considerable friction had been caused by people putting *their* papers into other people's pigeon-holes. On the opposite wall was an enormous shiny map of the world, with strange blue and red lines running across it. The third wall was filled with the fireplace, over which were two stern and dusty photographs of the Parthenon, Athens, and St. Peter's, Rome.

Although the air was sharp with the first early hint of autumn, the windows were open, and a little part of the garden could be seen—a gravel path down which golden-brown leaves were fluttering, a round empty flower-bed, a stone wall.

On the large table in the middle of the room tea was laid, one plate of bread and butter, and a plate of rock buns. Dormer, a round, red-faced, cheerful-looking person with white hair, aged about fifty, and Clinton, a short, athletic youth, with close-cropped hair and a large mouth, were drinking tea. Clinton had poured his into his saucer and was blowing at it—a practice that Perrin greatly disliked.

However, this was the first day of term, and

every one was very friendly. Perrin paused a moment in the doorway. 'Ah! here we are again!' he said with easy jocularity.

Dormer gave him a hand, and said, 'Glad to see you, Perrin; had good holidays?'

Clinton took the last rock bun, and shouted with a kind of roar, 'You old nut!'

Perrin, as he moved to the table, thought that it was a little hard that all the things that irritated him most should happen just when he was most inclined to be easy and pleasant.

'Ha! no cake!' he said, with a surprised air.

'Oh! I say, I'm so sorry,' said Clinton, with his mouth full, 'I took the last. Ring the bell.'

Perrin gulped down his annoyance, sat down, and poured out his tea. It was cold and leathery. Dormer was busily writing lists of names. The Lower School was divided into two houses—Dormer was house-master of one, and Perrin of the other. The other two junior men were under-house-masters: Clinton belonged to Dormer; and Traill, the new man, to Perrin. Both houses were in the same building, but the sense of rival camps gave a pleasant spur of emulation and competition both to work and play.

'I say, Perrin, have you made out your bath-lists? Then there are locker-names—I want . . .'

Perrin snapped at his bread and butter. 'Ah, Dormer, please—my tea first.'

'All right; only, it 's getting on to four.'

For some moments there was silence. Then

there came timid raps on the door. Perrin, in his most stentorian voice, shouted, 'Come in!'

The door slowly opened, and there might be seen dimly in the passage a misty cloud of white Eton collars and round, white faces. There was a shuffling of feet.

Perrin walked slowly to the door.

'Here we all are again! How pleasant! How extremely pleasant! All of us eager to come back, of course—um—yes. Well, you know you oughtn't to come now. Two minutes past four. I 'll take your names then—another five minutes. It 's up on the board. Well, Sexton? Hadn't you eyes? *Don't* you know that ten minutes past four *is* ten minutes past four and *not* four o'clock?'

'Yes, sir, please, sir—but, sir——'

Perrin closed the door, and walked slowly back to the fireplace.

'Ha, ha,' he said, smiling reflectively; 'had him there!'

Dormer was muttering to himself, 'Wednesday, 9 o'clock, Bilto, Cummin; 10 o'clock, Sayer, Long. Thursday, 9 o'clock——'

The golden leaves blew with a whispering chatter down the path.

The door opened again, and someone came in—Traill, the new man. Perrin looked at him with curiosity and some excitement. The first impression of him, standing there in the doorway, was of someone young and eager to make friends.

Someone young, by reason of his very dress—the dark brown Norfolk jacket, light grey flannel trousers, turned up and short, showing bright purple socks and brown brogues. His hair, parted in the middle and brushed back, was light brown; his eyes were brown and his cheeks tanned. His figure was square, his back broad, his legs rather short—he looked, beyond everything else, clean.

He stopped when he saw Perrin, and Dormer looked up and introduced them. Perrin was relieved that he was so young. Searle, last year, had been old enough to have an opinion of his own—several opinions of his own; he had contradicted Perrin on a great many points, and towards the end of the term they had scarcely been on speaking terms. Searle was a pig-headed ass. . . .

But Traill evidently wanted to 'know'—was quite humble about it, and sat, pulling at his pipe, whilst Perrin enlarged about lists and dormitories and marks and discipline to his heart's content. 'I must say as far as order goes I 've never found any trouble. It 's *in* a man if he 's going to do it—I 've always managed them all right—never any trouble—hum, ha! Yes, you 'll find them the first few days just a little restive—seeing what you 're made of, you know; drop on them, drop on them.'

Traill asked about the holiday task.

'Oh, yes, Dormer set that. *Ivanhoe*—Scott, you know. Just got to read out the questions, and see they don't crib. Let them go when you hear the chapel bell.'

Traill was profuse in his thanks.

'Not at all—anything you want to know.'

Perrin smiled at him.

There was, once again, the timid knock at the door. The door was opened, and a crowd of tiny boys shuffled in, headed by a larger boy who had the bold look of one who has lost all terror of masters, their ways, and their common rooms.

'Well, Sexton?' Perrin cleared his throat.

'Please, sir, you told me to bring the new boys. These are all I could find, sir—Pippin Minor is crying in the matron's room, sir.'

Sexton backed out of the room.

Perrin stared at the agitated crowd for some moments without saying anything. The boys were herded together like cattle, and were staring at him with eyes that started from their round, close-cropped heads. Perrin took their names down. Then he talked to them for three minutes about discipline, decency, and decorum; then he reminded them of their mothers, and finally said a word about serving their country.

Then he passed on to the subject of pocket-money. 'It will be safer for you to hand it over to me,' he said slowly and impressively. 'Then you shall have it when you want it.'

A slight shiver of apprehension passed through the crowd; then slowly, one by one, they delivered up their shining silver. One tiny boy—he had apparently no neck and no legs; he was very chubby—had only two half-crowns. He clutched these in his hot palm until Perrin said, 'Well, Rackets?'

Then, with his eyes fixed devouringly upon them, the boy delivered them up.

'I don't like to see you so fond of money, Rackets.' Perrin dropped the half-crowns slowly into his trouser pocket, one after the other. 'I don't think you will ever see these half-crowns again.' He smiled.

Rackets began to choke. His fist, which had closed again as though the money was still there, moved forward. A large, fat tear gathered slowly in his eye. He struggled to keep it back—he dug his fist into it, turned round, and fled from the room.

Perrin was amused. 'Caught friend Rackets on the hip,' he said.

Then suddenly, in the distance, an iron bell began to clang. The four men put on their gowns, gathered books together, and moved to the door. Traill hung back a little. 'You take the big room with me, Traill,' said Dormer. 'I 'll give you paper and blotting-paper.'

They moved slowly out of the room, Perrin last. A door was opened. There was a sudden cessation of confused whispers—complete silence, and then Perrin's voice: 'Question one. Who were Richard I, Gurth, Wamba, Brian-de-Bois-Guilbert? . . . B–r–i–a–n—hyphen . . .'

The door closed.

III

A few papers fluttered about the table. It was growing dark outside, and a silver moon showed above the dark mass of the garden wall.

The brown leaves, now invisible, passed rustling and whispering about the path. Into the room there stole softly, from the kitchen, the smell of onions. . . .

CHAPTER II

INTRODUCES A CONFUSING COMPANY OF PERSONS, WITH SPECIAL EMPHASIS ON MRS. COMBER

I

It would be fitting at this moment, were it possible, to give Traill's impressions, at the end of the first week, of the place and the people. But here one is met by the outstanding and dominating difficulty that Traill himself was not given to gathering impressions at all—he felt things, but he never saw them; he recorded opinions in simple language and an abbreviated vocabulary, but it was all entirely objective; motives, the way that things hung and were interdependent one upon the other, the sense of contrast and of the incessant jostling of comedy on tragedy and of irony upon both, never hit him anywhere.

Nevertheless, he had, in a clear, clean-cut way, his opinions at the end of the first week.

There is a letter of his to a college friend that is interesting, and there are some other things in a letter to his mother; but he was engaged, quite naturally, in endeavouring to keep up with the confusing medley of 'things to be done and things not to be done' that that first week must necessarily entail.

His relations to Perrin and Perrin's relations to him are, it may be said here now, once and for all, the entire *motif* of this episode—it is from first to last an attempt to arrive at a decision as to the real reasons of the catastrophe that ultimately occurred; and so, that being the case, it may seem that the particulars as to the rest of the people in the place, and, indeed, the place itself, are extraneous and unnecessary; but they all helped, every one of them, in their own way and their own time, to bring about the ultimate disaster, and so they must have their place.

Traill had learnt during his three years at Cambridge that, above all things, one must not worry. He had been inclined, a little at first, to think, after the easy indolence of Clifton, that one ought to bother. He had found that two-thirds in his Historical Tripos and a 'Blue' for Rugby football were very easily obtained; he found that the second of these things led to a popularity that invited a pleasant indifference to thought and discussion, and he was extremely happy.

His 'Blue' would undoubtedly have secured him something better than a post at Moffatt's had he taken more trouble; but he had left it, lazily, until the last, and had been forced to accept what he could get; in a term or two he hoped to return to Clifton.

All this meant that his stay at Moffatt's was in the nature of an interlude. He buoyantly looked upon it as a month or two of 'learning the ropes,' and he could not therefore be expected to regard masters, boys, or buildings with any very intense seriousness. It is, indeed, one of the most curious aspects of the whole affair that he remained, for so long a period, blind to all that was going on.

In his motives, in his actions, he was of a surprising simplicity. He found the world an entirely delightful place—there was Rugby football in the winter, and cricket in the summer; there were splendid walks; there was a week in town every now and again; as to people, there was his mother—a widow, and he was her only son—whom he entirely worshipped; there were one or two excellent friends of his from Clifton and Cambridge; there was no one whom he really disliked; and there were one or two girls, hazily, not very seriously, in the distance, whom he had liked very much indeed.

He read a little—liked it when he had time; had a passion for Napoleon, whose campaigns he had followed confusedly at Cambridge; and was even stirred—again when he had time—by certain sorts of poetry.

And it is this that leads me to one of the questions that are most difficult of decision—as to how strongly, if indeed at all, he had any feeling for beauty before he met Isabel Desart.

He certainly—if he had it at this time—could

not put it into words; but I believe that he had, in the back of his brain, a kind of consciousness about it all, and his meeting with Isabel fired what had been lying there waiting.

He never, certainly, talked about it, but it will be noticed that he went to the wood a great many times, even before he felt Isabel's influence, and that he realized quite vividly certain aspects of Pendragon and The Flutes; and he would not have cared for *Richard Feverel* quite so passionately had he not had something—some poetry and feeling—already in him.

The reverse of the shield is, at any rate, given in that first letter to his mother. He says of Moffatt's: 'You never saw anything so hideous. The red brick all looks so fresh, the stone corridors all smell so new, the iron and brass of the place is all so strong and regular. It 's like the labs. at Cambridge on an extensive scale; you 'd think they were inventing gases or something, not teaching boys the way they should go. . . . All the same, coming up the hill the other night, with the sun setting behind it, it looked quite black and grand--it 's the fresh-lobster colour of it that I can't stand. . . .'

That shows that he was, to some degree at any rate, sensitive to the way that the place looked, and he, in all probability, felt a great deal more about it than he ever said to any one.

Cambridge may have done something for him —few people can spend three years with those grey palaces and blue waters without some kind of development, although probably—because we are English—it is unconscious.

II

He had, during that first week, too much to do to get any very concrete idea of the staff. On the first morning of term there was a masters' meeting, and he could see them all sitting, heavily, despondently, in conclave. There was a gradation of seats, and Traill, of course, took the lowest—a little, hard, sharp one near the window with a shelf just above his head and it knocked him if he moved.

The Rev. Moy-Thompson, the head master—a venerable-looking clergyman, with a long grizzled beard and bony fingers—sat at the end of the table in an impatient way, as though he were longing for an excuse to fly into a temper. For the others, Traill only noticed one or two; Perrin, Dormer, and Clinton were there, of course. There was a large stout man with a heavy moustache and a sharp voice like a creaking door; a clergyman, thin and rather haggard, with a white wall of a collar much too big for him; an agitated little Frenchman, who seemed to expect that at any moment he might be the victim of a practical joke; a thin, bony little man with a wiry moustache and a biting, cynical speech that seemed to goad Moy-Thompson to fury;

a nervous and bald-headed man, whose hand continually brushed his moustache and whose manner was exceedingly deprecating. There were others, but these struck Traill's eyes as they roved about.

During the discussion that followed concerning the moving of boys up and the moving of boys down, the time of lock-up, the possibilities and disadvantages of the new boys, it seemed to be everybody's intention to be as unpleasant as possible under cover of an agreeable manncr. On several occasions it seemed that the storm was certain to break, and Traill bent eagerly forward in his seat; but the danger was averted.

As the week passed, he found that these men grew more distinct and individual. The stout man with the heavy moustache was called Comber; he had once been a famous football player, and was now engaged on a book concerning the athletes of Greece. The clergyman, the Rev. Stuart, was very quiet except on questions of ritual and ceremony, and these things stirred him into a passion. The little Frenchman, Monsieur Pons, spent his time in hating England and preparing to leave it—an escape that he never achieved.

The little man with the moustache, Birkland by name, seemed to Traill the most 'interesting' of them. He was fierce and caustic in his manner to everybody and was feared by the whole staff.

White, the nervous man, never, so far as Traill

could see, opened his mouth; and if he did say anything no one paid any attention to him.

None of these men, Traill discovered, concerned him very closely, as his work was for the most part at the Lower School. He was pleasant to all of them, and, if he had thought about it at all, would have said that they liked him; but he did not think about it.

His relations with Dormer, Perrin, and Clinton were quite agreeable. Dormer was kind and helpful in a fatherly way; Clinton admired his football and liked to compare Oxford (at which he had, several years before, been a shining light) with Traill's own university; Perrin asked him into his sitting-room for coffee and talked School Education to him at infinite length.

Every one, during this first week, quite pleasant and agreeable.

III

The ladies of the establishment came to Traill's notice more slowly; and they came to him, of course, considering his temperament, quite indefinitely and without his own immediate realization of anything. He could point, of course, to the moment of his meeting Isabel, because, from that moment, his life was changed; but it was the meeting rather than any keen and tangible idea of her that he realized.

It is essential, however, that Mrs. Comber

should appear on the scene a good deal more clearly than he would ever probably see her. She had so much to do with everything that occurred—quite unconsciously, poor lady, as indeed she was always unconscious of anything until it was over—that she demands a close attempt at accurate presentation.

The immediate impressions that she left on any observer, however casual, were of size and colour, and of all the things that go with those qualities. She was large, immense, and seemed from her movements and her air of rather tentatively and timidly embracing the world, to be even larger.

Her hair was of a blackness and her cheeks of a redness that hinted at foreign blood, but was derived in reality from nothing more than Cornish descent—and that indeed may, if you please, be taken as foreign enough. There was a great deal of hair piled on her head, and in her continual smiles and anxiety to be pleasant there seemed, too, to be a great deal of her red cheeks.

In those earlier days, the daughter of a country clergyman, and the youngest of six sisters, she had been, when so permitted, jolly, noisy, with a tremendous sense of life. The key that was going, she believed, to unlock life for her was Romance, and she looked eagerly and enthusiastically down the dusty road to watch for the coming of some knight. When he came in the person of Freddie Comber, young, handsome, athletic, and the most devout of lovers, she felt that, now that her lamp was lighted, she had only got to keep the flame burning and she would be happy for ever. That—the keeping of it alight—seemed, as she looked at the handsome and ardent Freddie, an easy enough thing to do. She did not know that Fate very often, having given a tempting glimpse and even a positive handling of its burnished brass and intricate tracing, removes it altogether—merely, as it may seem to some cynical observers of life, for the fun of the thing. In any case, from the moment of her marriage, Mrs. Comber's eager hands found nothing to hold on to at all, and she passed in the ensuing years from a plucky determination to make the 'second best' do to the final blind acquiescence in anything at all that might have the faintest resemblance to that earlier glorious radiance.

Freddie Comber's transition from the handsome, enthusiastic young lover into the stout, lethargic and querulous Mr. Comber, master of the Middle Fourth and anticipatory author of a work on the athletes of Greece, would need an exhaustive treatise on 'Public School Education as applied to our Masters' for its reasonable analysis. Perhaps this faithful account of the relations of Perrin and Traill may offer some solution to that and other more complex riddles.

It says, however, everything for Mrs. Comber's

pluck and determined stupidity that she lived, even now, after fifteen years' married life, at the threshold of expectation. Things that were apparent to the complete stranger in his first five minutes' interview with Comber were hidden, wilfully and proudly hidden, from *her*.

She yielded to facts, however, in this one particular, that she extended her attempts at Romance to wider fields. It always might return as far as Freddie was concerned—she was continually hoping and expecting that it would; but meanwhile she dug diligently in other grounds. Her three boys—fat, stolid, stupid, pugnacious—cared, they showed her quite plainly, nothing for her at all; but she put that down to their age, to their school, even to their appetites, their clothes, anything that pointed to a probable change in the future. In their holidays she spent her days in eagerly loving them and being repulsed, and then in hiding her love under a troubled indifference and being entirely disregarded. . . . They were unpleasant boys.

Another place for digging was the ground of 'things,' of property. Having had nothing at all when she was a girl, and having almost nothing—they were very poor, and she 'managed' badly—now, she had always had an intense feeling for possession. She was generous to an amazing degree, and would give anything, in her tangled, impetuous kind of way, to anybody without a moment's thought. But she loved her valuables.

They were very few. Potatoes and cabbages, clothing and school-bills for the boys, consumed any money that there might happen to be, and consumed it in a muddled, helpless kind of way that she was never able to prevent or correct. But things had come to her — been given, left, or eagerly seized in a wild moment's extravagance —and these she cherished with all her eyes and hands. The peacock-blue Liberty screen, the ormolu clock, some few pieces of dainty Dresden china, some brass Indian pots, a small but musically charming piano, some sketches and two good prints, an *édition de luxe* of Walter Pater (a wedding present, and she had never opened one of these beautiful volumes), some silver, a teapot, a tray, some cups that Freddie had won in an earlier, more glorious period, some small pieces of jewellery—over these things she passed every morning with a delicate, lingering touch.

Clumsy and awkward as she generally was, when she approached her valuables she became another person: she would lie awake thinking about them. . . . They seemed—dumb things as they were—to give her something of the affection for which, from more eloquent persons, she was always so continually searching.

She was as clumsy in her relations to all her neighbours and acquaintances as she was in her movements and her finances. She was famous for her want of tact; famous, too, for a certain coarseness and bluntness of speech; famous for a childlike and transparent attempt to make people like her—an attempt that, from its transparency, always with wiser and more cynical persons failed.

She generally thought of three things at once and tried to talk about them all; she was quite aware that most of the ladies connected with the town and the neighbourhood disliked her, and she never, although she wondered in a kind of muddled dismay why it was, could discover a satisfactory reason. She spent her years in cheerfully rushing into people's lives and being hurriedly bundled out again—which 'bundling,' at every reiteration of it, left her as confused and dismayed as before.

But against all this rejection and muddled confusion there was, of course, to be set Isabel Desart. What Miss Desart was to Mrs. Comber no simple succession of printed words can possibly say. She was, in her free, spontaneous fashion, a great many things to a great many people; but to none of them was she quite the special and wonderful gift that she was to Mrs. Comber.

Perhaps it was some feeling of this kind that brought her so often, and for so long a period, down to Moffatt's—a proceeding that her London friends could never even vaguely understand. That she—having, as she might, such a glorious 'time' in London behind her—should care to go and stay for so long a period at that dullest of places, a school, with those dullest and most arid of people, scholastic authorities (this term to include wives as well as husbands), was indeed to them all a total mystery.

Mrs. Comber, with all her faults and insufficiences, would have seemed a poor enough answer to the riddle as an answer; it was, in fact, only partial.

In addition to Mrs. Comber there was Cornwall; and Cornwall, as it was at Moffatt's, was quite enough to draw Isabel unerringly, irresistibly.

Of the place—the surroundings, the look of it all, the 'sense' of it—there is more to be said in a moment—being seen, more completely perhaps, with Traill's new and unaccustomed eyes; it is enough here that, on every separate occasion of her coming, it meant to Isabel deeper and more vital experiences. She was beginning even to be afraid that it was not going to let her go again: its sea, its hard, black rocks, its golden gorge, its deep green lanes, its grey-roofed cottages that nestled in bowls and cups of colour as no cottages nestle anywhere else in the world—these were all things that she dreamed of afterwards, when she had left them, to the extent, it began to seem to her, of danger and confusion.

She herself 'fitted in' as only a few people out of the many that go there could ever do.

With her rather short brown hair that curled about her head, her straight eyes, her firm mouth, her vigorous, unerring movements, the swing of her arms as she walked, she seemed as though her strength and honesty might forbid her softer graces. To most people she was a delightful boy—splendidly healthy, direct, uncompromising, sometimes startling in her hatred of things and people, sometimes arrogant in her assured enthusiasms; Mrs. Comber, who, in her muddled, eager way, had told her so much, knew of the other side of her, of her tenderness, her understanding.

The boys loved her, and she had been their envoy on many occasions of peril and disaster; they always trusted her to carry things through, and she generally did.

It was only, perhaps, with the other ladies of the establishment that she did not altogether find favour. The other ladies consisted of Mrs. Moy-Thompson, Mrs. Dormer, and the lady matrons—Miss Bonhurst, the two Misses Madder, and Miss Tremans.

Mrs. Moy-Thompson, a thin, faded lady in perpetual black, had long ago been crushed into a miserable negligibility by her masterful husband. She very seldom spoke at all, and, when she did, hurriedly corrected what she had just said in a sudden fear lest she should be misunderstood. She allowed her husband to bully her to his heart's content.

Mrs. Dormer, stern, with the manner of one who never says what she means, had never got over the disappointment of her husband having, fifteen years before, missed the headmastership. She was continually finding new reasons for this omission and venting her dislike on people who had had nothing whatever to do with it. She was neat and puritanical, and hated Mrs. Comber because she was neither of these things.

Of the matrons, it may be enough to say that they all disliked each other, but were perfectly ready to combine in their mutual dislike of the other ladies; they felt that their position demanded that they should assert their birth and breeding; they also felt that Mrs. Comber and Mrs. Dormer looked down on them.

The best of them was the matron of the Lower School, the elder Miss Madder—stout and kind-hearted and extremely capable. She made up for the undeniable fact that no one had ever asked her to change her name for a pleasanter one by loving the small boys of the Lower School with a warmth and good-humour that they none of them, in after life, forgot.

And so there they all were—most of them—a background, and simply, as individuals, witnesses to the whole case and, perhaps, by reason of their very existence, factors in assisting the result.

They were, most of them, never in young Traill's consciousness at all—Miss Madder, perhaps because she was at the Lower School; Mrs. Comber, because Isabel was staying with her . . . and Isabel.

IV

A word, finally, about the surrounding country. It becomes, perhaps, at once most definitely presented if you take the Brown Hill as the centre, and Pendragon to the right along the coast, and Truro inland to the left—both at an equal distance—as the farthest boundaries.

Between Truro and Moffatt's there is a ridge of hill—undulating gently, vaguely shaped, with its cool brown colours melting into the blue or grey of the sky as dim clouds melt into one another.

The Brown Hill itself rises sharply, steeply, straight from the sea, with the little village—Chattock—at its feet, curling with its steep, cobbled street up the incline. Half-way down the hill there is a wood—the Brown Wood—and it hangs with all its feathery trees in friendly, eager fashion over the little white-stoned and yellow-sanded cove (so tiny and so perfect in its shape and colour that it almost audibly cries out not to be touched). There is a little part of the wood where the trees part and you may sit, in a kind of magical wonder, right over the grey carpet of the sea, hearing what the wood, with its creaking and bending and rustling, is saying to the water and what the water, with its slipping and hissing and singing, is saying to the wood. Of the two towns Pendragon has become, from the invasion of the Vandals, modern and monotonous.

It had, not so long ago, a cove on its outskirts—that was the whole of Cornwall in a tiny space; now there is a row of modern villas, red-roofed and wooden-paled. Traill, in his visits there, was concerned with the chief house there—The Flutes, owned by a certain Sir Henry Trojan, whose son, Robin Trojan, had been, although senior, a friend at Cambridge. The house was beautiful both in its position and in the spirit of its owner, and Traill snatched what moments he could to visit it and to snatch a respite there.

Had he known, it became in the back of his mind a contrast with the 'lobster red' and the stone corridors of Moffatt's, so that he took its wide, high rooms and its shining, ordered garden with an added sense of richness. Had he realized how soon its dignity and peace stood to him for an 'escape,' he would have realized also his growing protest against his voluntary imprisonment. He went over also on occasions to Truro—because he liked the walk over the hill, because he liked certain quaintnesses in the market, in the sharp cobbles of Lemon Street, in the higher breezes of Kenwyn, because, above all, he liked the grey quiet and solemnity of the Cathedral.

The point about both Pendragon and Truro is that it was the kind of life that he was leading at Moffatt's—the sides of it that are soon to be given you in detail—that led him to notice these places. Contrast drove him to a sudden opening of his eyes—contrast and Isabel Desart. He was growing so very quickly.

In letters to his mother he spoke of a splendid little wood where one could sit and watch the sea for hours if there was only time: of the funny old hill, all brown, with the white road curling up it; of calling at The Flutes, and 'Sir Henry Trojan and Lady Trojan being most awfully kind,' and the house being quite beautiful, but very little about the people of the school, and during those first weeks nothing at all about Isabel Desart.

It was not until Mrs. Comber gave her dinner-party that the preliminaries could be said to be over.

CHAPTER III

CONCERNS ALL THE WONDERFUL THINGS THAT MAY HAPPEN BETWEEN SOUP AND DESSERT

I

When Mrs. Comber asked Vincent Perrin to her dinner-party he was delighted, although he assumed as great an indifference as possible. This was at the end of the first week of term, and he had not spoken to Miss Desart—he had merely bowed to her across the grass and gone indoors to teach the Lower Third algebra with a beating heart.

He was also fortunately prevented from seeing that Mrs. Comber was giving the dinner for Traill. If he had seen that, things might have been very different; as it was, he thought that that kind, good-natured woman (he did not always like her) had noticed his attachment—as he thought most carefully concealed—to Miss Desart and wanted to help him.

He himself had not noticed the attachment until the holidays. She had stayed at Moffatt's during part of the summer term, and he had played tennis with her and talked to her and even walked with her. But it was not until he had returned to the seclusion of his aged mother and Buckinghamshire that he realized that for the first time for twenty years he was in love.

The discovery affected him in many ways. In the first place it swept away in the most curious manner all the years that had intervened since the last affair. He was suddenly young again. He began to regret the way that he had spent his days. He played tennis (badly but with enthusiasm). He talked to the men of his club about 'the absurdity of considering forty-five any age,' and quoted juvenile athletes of eighty. He gave his moustache a terrible time, wearing things to hold it straight at night, looking at it often in the glass.

He told his aged mother (a very old lady with a brown, shrivelled face, a white lace cap, and mittens) vaguely but magnificently about there being somebody. He hinted that she cared for him and was eager to marry him as soon as he felt ready to ask her. He talked about 'getting a house,' even about wall-papers and stair-carpets and a nice sunny room for the old lady.

She was delighted at first, and then agitated. Who might this new young person be? Perhaps she would not like her—in any case it meant taking a second place. But she idolized and worshipped her son: she knew sides of him that no one else knew—she saw him as a little, thin, serious boy in knickerbockers.

But this new spirit revived things in Vincent

Perrin that he had long thought dead. He knew, he savagely knew, in his heart of hearts, that he was a failure; he was determined that the world should never know it; he covered his knowledge with a multitude of disguises; but now perhaps, if she cared for him, there might yet be a chance.

But most of all he was afraid of something—he could never give it a name—that always crept slowly, increasingly over him as term advanced. He could not give it a name: that thing made up of a myriad details, of a myriad vexations; that evil spirit that they all, the masters and the rest, seemed to feel as the weeks gathered in numbers—the end-of-termy feelings: strained nerves, irritated tempers, almost, the last week or two when examinations came, seeing red.

No—this term it *shall* be all right. He felt, as he said good-bye to his mother and kissed her, almost an eagerness to get back and prove that it was all right. After all, Searle had left, and there was Miss Desart. Supposing she cared for him? He twisted his thin fingers together. Oh! what things he could do!

And so he was glad of Mrs. Comber's dinner-party.

II

Giving a dinner-party was no light, easy thing for Mrs. Comber. So many wide issues were involved. Not very many dinner-parties were given during the term, and Mrs. Comber was perfectly aware of all the conversation to which it would give rise, of all the people that would in all probability be angry with all the other people because they had been asked or because they had not. There was, generally, a reason for a dinner. Some important person had to be asked, some unimportant people had to be worked off, someone was conscious that there had not been a dinner-party for a very long time. But on this occasion there was no reason except that Mrs. Comber had liked the look of young Traill, had at once thought of Isabel, and had conceived a plan.

Then, of course, it followed that other people must be asked: Vincent Perrin, because she didn't like him, but felt that she ought to; the Dormers, because it was time they were asked; and the elder Miss Madder, because she was the nicest of the matrons and wouldn't talk quite so much and quite so spitefully as the others would.

All this involved danger and destruction as far as the people invited were concerned. One chance word at dinner—some errant, tiny omission or commission—and anything might happen: the time might be made miserable for everybody.

But there was more immediate peril in it than that. There was in the first place 'ways and means.' How this harassed poor Mrs. Comber no words can say. She was forced to drive her frail cockle-shell of a boat between the Scylla of increased bills and the Charybdis of not-being-smart-enough.

Were things not right—if there were no meringues, no mushroom savouries (there were rules and regulations about these things)—well, the party had better not be given at all. And then, on the other hand, there was the end of the month, nothing in hand to pay, and Freddie scowling over his *Greek Athletes* to such an extent that it wouldn't do to speak to him. All this was dreadfully difficult, but it revolved in reality almost entirely around Freddie's stout figure. Every dinner-party, every party of any kind, was an attempt to win Freddie back.

Mrs. Comber never confessed this even to herself, and she was, poor woman, only too completely aware that its usual result was to drive Freddie only more completely 'in.' Something was sure to happen, before the evening was over, to annoy him—she would have 'such a time afterwards.' But it always, of course, might be the other way. He might suddenly see, by some little word or act, how fond, how terribly fond, she was of him. She had learnt Bridge to please him—he used to like a game; but the result, although she would not admit it, had simply been disastrous.

She was much too muddled a person to be good at cards—she was very, very bad; she lost sixpences and shillings with the sinking feeling in her heart that they ought to be going to pay for their boys' clothes. She plunged desperately to win it all back again—she was known throughout the neighbourhood as the worst player in the world.

It was indeed this conclusion to the evening that she dreaded most of all. There were eight of them, so, of course, they would have to play. Her heart sank because of all the things that might happen.

But Isabel was, of course, the greatest use in the world. She saved all kinds of needless extravagances; she always got things where they were cheap and not bad, instead of getting them expensive and rotten. She thought of a thousand little things, and she managed the servants—only two of them and both ill-tempered.

Mrs. Comber said nothing to Isabel about young Traill—she did not even think that she had as yet noticed him. They neither of them said a word about Mr. Perrin.

III

Gathered all together in the drawing-room, it was everybody's chief object to avoid knocking things over. This may be taken metaphorically as well as literally, but in that ten minutes' prelude every one had the hard task of being socially agreeable to people whom they met, as they met their tables and their chairs, their beds and their hair-brushes, every day of their lives.

The curtains had been closely drawn, but outside the winds were up and were beating with wild fingers at the panes. They gathered in clusters about the house, screamed in derision at the dinner-party, chattered wildly round the buttresses and chimneys of the sedate and solemn buildings, and then rushed furiously down the gravel paths and away to the sea.

The tall lamp had been so placed that its light fell on the peacock-blue screen and the ormolu clock; it also fell on the enormous shoulders, in black silk, of Miss Madder, on the thin, bony neck of Mrs. Dormer, and on the deep red of Mrs. Comber's dress (open at one place at the back, where it should have been closed, and cut, Mrs. Dormer considered, a great deal lower than it need have been).

They were all waiting for Mr. Comber, and Mrs. Comber was trying to explain to Traill why Freddie was always late, why people at Moffatt's always liked meringues, and why with a magnificent 'heart' hand she had, only two nights ago, gone hearts with the most disastrous results. 'They like them best with jam in them—you shall see to-night if they aren't good; and there was really no reason at all why they shouldn't have come off, but we had such bad luck, and I oughtn't to have played my king when I did; I 'm always telling him that he ought to go and dress a little earlier—but he stays working.'

Poor Mrs. Comber! She was talking with

her eyes all about the room, with a sickening consciousness that something was wrong with her dress at the back, with a sure and a certain knowledge that it would be related in the common room the next morning that dinner was kept half an hour too long, with a keen misgiving that Mrs. Dormer and Miss Madder had quarrelled furiously only the day before and that she had known nothing about it. Every now and again she glanced at Isabel to gather comfort from her, and Isabel's eyes were always ready to give it her.

Isabel was standing in a dark corner by the window, talking to Vincent Perrin. Her dress was of dark silk, very simply cut, and falling in one straight piece, save for a golden girdle that bound her waist. She was standing with that perfect repose that came to her so naturally; when she moved it was as though that was the only movement possible—her limbs did not seem to hesitate, as do the limbs of so many people, before they could decide on the way that they were going to act. Her brown eyes were smiling at Vincent Perrin in a very friendly way, and his heart was beating a great deal faster than it had ever beaten before.

He had taken very especial pains with his dressing that night. He found that there were only three shirts in his drawer and that the cuffs of two of them were badly frayed, and that the stud-hole in the third was so broken that it would need a very large stud indeed to fill it. He found a kind of soup-plate at last, but was painfully conscious of its brazen size and of a little brown smudge on the front of the shirt near the collar. His suit—it had done duty for a great many years—was painfully shiny in the back: he had never noticed it before; and there was a small tear in one sleeve that he knew every one would see. His hair, in spite of water, was lanky and uneven; his moustache was raggeder than ever; his coat sleeves fell over his cuffs and shot them into obscurity in the most distressing manner.

All these things were new discomforts and distresses—he had never cared about them before. Then, when Isabel was so kind to him, he felt that they did not matter; he began in another few minutes to believe that he was rather well dressed after all; after ten minutes' conversation he was proud of his appearance.

Then suddenly his eye fell on Traill, and that moment must be recorded as the first instant of his dislike. Traill was absurd, quite absurd—over-dressed, in fact.

His hair was brushed and parted so that you could almost see your face in brown glossiness. His coat fitted amazingly. There was a wonderful white waistcoat with pearl buttons, there were wonderful silk socks with pale blue clocks, there was a splendid even line of white cuff below the sleeves.

But Perrin was forced to admit that this smartness was not common; it was quite natural, as though Traill had always worn clothes like that. Could it be that Perrin was shabby . . . *not* that Traill was smart?

Perrin dragged his cuffs from their dark hiding-places, then saw that there was a new frayed piece that had escaped his scissors, and pushed them back again.

They all went in to dinner.

IV

Traill took Isabel in. That was the first time that she had consciously recognized him—even then it was fleeting and was confined in reality to a vague approval . . . and she liked his voice.

He had never seen her before—that is, he had never detached her from the vague background of people moving in the distance against the trees and the buildings; but now at once he fell in love with her. He had been in love before, and the strange suddenness of the ending of those fugitive episodes—the way that it had been, in an instant, like a candle blown out—had led him to fancy that love was always like that; he had even begun to be a little cynical about it. But he was in no way a complicated person. It didn't seem to him in the least strange that yesterday he should have laughed at love and that now he should have a sense of beauty and strange wonder—something that had suddenly, like streaming silk or a sweeping, golden sunlight, flooded Mrs. Comber's dining-room.

He thought her very grave; he noticed the white, crinkly sound of the silk of her dress against the table, the light in her curly hair, and the way that her fingers, so slim and soft and yet so strong, touched the white cloth; and when she asked him whether he had ever been a schoolmaster before, the soup suddenly choked him and he could not answer her, but blushed like a fool, waving a spoon.

'And you like it?'

'I *love* it.'

'So far. Well, you shall cherish your illusions.' She still looked at him very gravely. 'The boys like you.'

'Ah! they told you!' He was pleased at that.

'Oh! one soon knows—they are cruelly frank.'

Suddenly she caught her eyes away from him and looked down the table. Mrs. Comber was in distress. Every one had finished their soup a long time before, and there was no sign of the fish. One of those pauses that are so cruelly eloquent fell about the table. Freddie Comber was moodily staring at his plate and paying no attention at all to Dormer, who was trying to be pleasant. Mrs. Dormer was sitting up stiffly in her chair and gazing at Landseer's 'Dignity and Impudence,' that hung on the opposite wall, as though she had never seen it before.

It was at moments like this that Mrs. Comber felt as though the room got up and hit one in the face. She was always terribly conscious of her dining-room. It was a room, she felt, 'with nothing at all in it.' It had a wall-paper that she hated; she had always intended to have a new one, but there had never been quite enough money to spend on something that was not, after all, a necessity. The Landseer picture offended her, although she could give no reason—perhaps she did not care about dogs. The sideboard was a dreadfully cheap one, with imitation brass knobs to the doors of the cupboards, and there were three shelves of dusty and tattered books that never got cleared away.

All these things seemed to rise and scream at her. She noticed, too, with a little pang of dismay, that one of the glass dessert dishes was missing. The set had been one of their wedding presents—the nicest present that they had had. Oh! those servants! . . . She talked with a brave smile to anybody and everybody, but she watched furtively her husband's gloomy face.

But Isabel, having given her a smile, turned back and attacked Mr. Perrin, feeling, as she always did about him, that she was sorry for him, that she wanted to be kind to him, and that she would be so glad when her duty would be over. She also noticed that she wanted to talk to Traill again.

Perrin himself had been in a state of torture

during dinner that was, for him, an entirely new experience. Traill had taken her in. . . . His thoughts hung about this fact as bees hang about a tree. Traill—Traill . . . with his elegant waistcoat and his beautiful shirt. He splashed his soup on to his plate. As through a mist people's words came to him—Miss Madder's fat, cheerful voice: 'Oh! I think we shall fill the West Dormitory this term. There are five small Newsoms—all new boys, poor dears.' . . . Comber himself, growling at the end of the table to Dormer: 'It's perfectly absurd. It means that Birkland has one hour less than the rest of us—that middle hour ten to eleven . . .'

The same old subjects, the same old dinners—but with her he was going to escape from it all; with her by his side, his ambition would grow wings.

He saw himself at Eton or Harrow, or a school-inspectorship. Why not? He was able enough. It only needed something to force him out of the rut.

But Traill had taken her in. . . .

And then she turned and spoke to him, and at once he put up his hand as though he would stroke his chin, but really it was to cover the stud—the large soup-plate stud. He stroked his straggling moustache, and used his official voice. He spoke as he always did when he wanted to create an impression, as though in the cloistral courts of Cambridge.

Slow, deliberate, a little majestic . . . he shot his cuff back into his sleeve. He spoke of ambition, of the things that a man could do if he tried, of the things that *he* could do, if——

'If?' said Isabel.

'Oh! well, if . . . marriage, for instance, was such a help to a man . . . one never knew——' He drank furiously and finished at a gulp a glass of Freddie Comber's very bad claret.

Young Traill was having a very good time indeed with Miss Madder, and Isabel turned round to hear what they were talking about. The meringues had arrived—there was also fruit-salad, but every one took meringues, although they would have liked, had they dared, to take both—and conversation was quite lively.

'I do hope,' said Mrs. Dormer, 'that there will be several extra halves this term.'

And at once poor Mrs. Comber, who was eagerly congratulating herself on the success with which, so far, she had escaped danger, burst in:

'Oh, so do I. You know, they always used to give the boys a half for every new baby born on the establishment. Well, you and I have done our duty nobly in that direction, haven't we, Mrs. Dormer?'

It is impossible that those who are not acquainted with both ladies should have any conception of the disaster that this simple sentence involved.

Mrs. Dormer had a glorious, pugnacious prudery in her stiff, angular body that rejoiced in any opportunity for display. She hated Mrs. Comber; she had now an excuse of offence for weeks.

She could embroider and discuss to her heart's delight. She saw in the amusement of Miss Madder, the discomfort of her husband, the dismay of Miss Desart, the distaste of Mr. Perrin, the wrath of Mr. Comber, ample confirmation of her exultant prophecies. It does not take much to make a scandal at Moffatt's—and the propriety of the schoolmaster, the anxious, eager propriety, exceeds the propriety of every other profession.

Mrs. Dormer had the game in her hands, and she played the first move by sitting silently, whitely, protestingly in her chair.

'I *do* hope the football will be good this season,' she said at last, quietly and patiently, to Mr. Comber.

Mrs. Comber realized at once that she was defeated. She did not know why she had said a thing like that—she knew that Mrs. Dormer didn't like such things to be talked about. She smiled and laughed and talked about gardens and the school bell and Mrs. Moy-Thompson's hat. 'It always rings half a note flat, and it's no use speaking about it; and how she can bear that coloured green when it's the last colour she *ought* to wear, I *can't* think; if it weren't for these flies—what do you call them?—the roses would have done quite well.' But her eyes stared desperately down the table at Freddie, and she saw that he would not look at her, and she knew that the dinner had been only one more nail in her coffin.

There was still, of course, Bridge.

V

Sitting at the little tables in the tiny drawing-room afterwards, they were all tremendously—as of course you must be at such small tables—conscious of each other.

They had drawn lots, and Mrs. Comber was playing with Dormer against her husband and Miss Madder at one table, and Mr. Perrin was playing with Mrs. Dormer against Isabel and young Traill at another.

It may seem a slight thing, but it was certainly a factor in the whole situation that Perrin was forced to gaze—over a very small intervening space—at Traill's immaculate clothes for the rest of the evening. He was always a bad Bridge player—he thought that he disguised his bad play by a haughty manner and a false assurance; to-night the confusion of his thoughts, his incipient dislike for Traill, the bad claret that he had drunk, the distracting way that Miss Desart held her cards, caused his play to be something insane.

Mrs. Dormer disliked intensely losing money, and there seemed every prospect, if Perrin continued to play like that, of her losing at least five shillings before the end of the evening. She was convinced that she had every reason for being angry, and when, at the end of the first deal, her partner had thrown away a splendid heart hand by refusing to follow any of her leads, she could not resist a stiff movement in her chair and a sharp 'Well, Mr. Perrin, I think we ought to have done better than that.'

For the first time in his experience his usual assured reply, containing an implication that it was all his partner's fault, that he had been at Cambridge for three years, and that he taught Algebra and Euclid six days a week and therefore ought to know how to play Bridge if any one did, failed him. He stared at her miserably, gathered the cards hurriedly together, and began to shuffle them in a dreadfully confused way. He knew that Miss Desart must think him a fool, and he wanted her so terribly badly to think him clever and even brilliant. He was sure that Traill was laughing at him. He hated the assurance with which he played. If only he, Perrin, had been playing with Miss Desart what things he might have done! . . . His head ached, and his shirt creaked a little every time he moved, and every time it creaked Mrs. Dormer made a little stir of disapproval.

At the other table also things were not as they should be. The drawing of lots had secured precisely the combination of players that Mrs. Comber had most wished to avoid. Whatever she did, however she played, she was lost. If she played badly, her husband, although playing against her, was infuriated at her stupidity; if she won, he hated being beaten. As it was, she was playing extremely badly, but was winning because of the good cards that she held. His brow was growing blacker and blacker. She held her cards so badly —she never could make them into a fan, and every now and again one fell with a sharp rattle against the table.

Also she forgot sometimes that they were playing and broke into sentences that had to be instantly checked—as, for instance: 'Oh, I saw Mrs. . . . I 'm so sorry, it 's my lead.' 'I believe *this* term . . . Oh! I beg your pardon. . . . *What* are trumps?'

Every now and again she gazed at the peacock screen, and the clock, and the dark corner of the room where there was a little water-colour in a gilt frame, and they gave her comfort.

The end of the rubber came, and Mrs. Dormer refused to play any more; they had had magnificent cards, but she had lost three shillings. She wouldn't look at Mr. Perrin. He stood nervously moving one foot against the other, pulling his moustache.

'No, really I 'm afraid we must go. You 've finished your rubber, Mrs. Comber? Yes, we *ought* to have won. . . . No, I can't think how it was.'

'Considering the way my wife 's been playing,' said Freddie Comber brutally, 'I think it is just as well to stop.'

Mrs. Comber chattered with amazing confusion

as she helped Mrs. Dormer to get her cloak. In her eyes something bright was shining, and every now and again she put up her hand to push back some of her black hair (always on the edge of a perilous descent) with a little desperate action.

'Good night. I'm so glad you've enjoyed it. We meet to-morrow, of course, although I can't think why they aren't going to play golf—there's going to be such a storm in an hour or two, isn't there?—probably because it's football to-morrow afternoon. Yes, good-bye.'

Every one departed. Mr. Perrin stood desperately with something going up and down in his throat. He had a sentence in his head: 'Please, Miss Desart, *do* let me see you back to the lodge.' (Mrs. Comber had had to plant her out there to sleep because there was no room in their own tiny house.) He meant to say it, he wanted to say it. He clutched his mortar-board frantically in his hand. Then suddenly he heard Traill's voice:

'Oh! please, Miss Desart—of course, I'll see you back. Good night, Mrs. Comber. Thank you *so* much—I've *loved* it. Good night, Comber. Night, Perrin. Look out, Miss Desart, it's dark.'

Perrin felt his hand just touched by Miss Desart's, and her voice, 'Good night, Mr. Perrin.'

He was left alone on the step.

VI

I don't suppose that at this stage of things Isabel had the very slightest idea of all the emotions that had been in play that evening. Her head, as they walked away down the dark gravel path, was full of her hostess.

'Poor Mrs. Comber,' she said, and then checked herself as though there were some disloyalty in talking about her. 'I hate Mrs. Dormer,' she added quietly.

'I don't like her,' Traill said. 'And Dormer 's such a jolly little man. I don't envy him.'

'Oh! I don't suppose it 's her fault any more than it 's any one's fault here about anything they do. It 's all a case of nerves.'

There was going to be a storm soon. Already that little preparatory whisper of the wind, the ominous, frightened rustle of the leaves down the path, was about them. It was all very dark, with a curious white light on the horizon, and the buildings of the Lower School huddled against it in sharp, black outline like the broad backs of giants bending to the soil.

The scent of trees—vague and uncertain in the daytime, but now clear and pungent—was borne through the air, and the voice of the sea, rolling in long mournful cadences far below the hills, came up to them. The wind's whisper grew into a furious, strangled cry; little eddies of it swept about their feet, and cascades of withered leaves fell wildly against them and were blown, sweeping, streaming away.

They were silent. Traill was thinking of her voice. It was so grave and assured and restful. He thought that he could trust her tremendously. But there was reserve in it too, and he felt, a little hopelessly, that he might never perhaps get to know her better.

When they got to the lodge gates, they stopped and stood for a moment in silence.

Then she said, looking very gravely in front of her at the dark bend of the road: 'There must be such a storm coming up. I feel it all through me. It *was* depressing to-night, wasn't it?'

'Just a little,' he said.

'Anyhow, I'm glad you like it—being here. Mind you always do. I don't want to be pessimistic when you are just beginning; but—well, you don't mean to stay here for ever, do you?'

'I should think not,' he answered eagerly. 'Only a term or two at the most, and then I hope to go back to Clifton, my old school.'

'That's right—because—really it isn't a very good place to be—this.'

'Why not?' he asked.

'It's difficult to explain without maligning people and making things out worse than they really are.' She paused a moment and then she went on: 'Do you know, at the bottom of the hill, just before you get into the village, a melancholy orchard? One always passes it. You will see at the right time of the year lots of green apples on the trees, but they never seem to come to anything. And such blossom in the spring! I 've seen men working there sometimes. I don't know what it is, but nothing 's any good there. They call it in the village "Green Apple Orchard." . . . Well, I 've stayed here a great deal, and there 's an obvious comparison.'

'That 's cheerful,' he said, laughing. 'It would, I suppose, be awful if one had to stay here for ever like Perrin and Dormer and the rest of them; but this time next year will see me somewhere better, I hope.'

'Mind you stick to that,' she said eagerly. 'I have a horrible kind of feeling that they all meant to go very soon; but here they are still —soured, disappointed. Oh, it doesn't bear thinking of.'

'One must have ambition,' he answered her confidently.

She smiled at him, and took his hand, and said good night.

He went, smiling, to his room. As he climbed into bed, the storm broke furiously.

CHAPTER IV

BIRKLAND LOQUITUR

I

AT the end of his first month young Traill looked back, as it were from the top of a hill, and thought that it all had been very pleasant. How much of this pleasantness was due to Isabel (although he had seen her during that period extremely seldom) and how much of it was due to his agreeable acceptance of things as they were without any very definite challenge to them to be different, it is impossible to say.

The crowded day had of course something to do with it; the fact that there was never, from the first harsh clanging of the bell down the stone passages at half-past six to the last leap into bed, jumping as it were from a heap of Latin exercises and the cold challenge of Perrin's voice as he went round the dormitories turning lights out—never a moment's pause to think about anything extra at all. But he was in no way a reflective person. He saw that his own small boys in their untidy, scrambling kind of way liked him and that the bigger boys of the Upper Fourth, to whom he taught French twice a week, revered him because of his football.

The masters at the Upper School seemed pleasant fellows, although he might, had he thought about it, have perceived dimly an atmosphere of unrest and discomfort in their common room.

With Moy-Thompson as yet he had had no dealings at all. He had been to supper there once on Sunday night, had been appalled by the dreariness of the whole affair, the shrivelled ill-temper of Moy-Thompson's parents (aged about ninety apiece), the inadequacy of the food, the melancholy inertia of Mrs. Moy-Thompson; but he had had no nearer relations with him.

He had, indeed, already begun to perceive that in his own common room things were not quite as they should be. He was always an exceedingly equable and easy-tempered person, and he had been surprised at himself on several occasions for being irritated at very unimportant and insignificant details. There were, for instance, the incidents of the bath and the morning papers. Both of these incidents derived their irritation from their original connection with Perrin, and this might have led him, had he thought about it, to the discovery that he did not like Perrin and that Perrin did not like him. But he never dwelt upon things—he was always thinking of the matter immediately in hand, and when there was an empty reflective quarter of an hour his eyes were on Isabel.

The incident of the bath was, it might have been thought, inconsiderable.

Perrin's bedroom was next to Traill's. Opposite their doors, on the other side of the passage, was a bathroom containing two baths. In this bathroom Traill always arrived some minutes after Perrin. Try as he might, he never succeeded in arriving first. Perrin always filled both baths, one with hot and one with cold, and stood moodily, his naked body gaunt and bony in the grey light, watching them whilst they filled. Traill was forced to wait until Perrin had had both his baths before he could have his. At first it had seemed a small matter. Gradually as the days passed the irritation grew. There was something in Perrin's complacent immobility as he stood above his bath that was of itself annoying. Why should a man wait? One morning they rushed out together. There were words.

'I say, Perrin, why not have hot and cold in the same bath?'

'Really, Traill, it isn't, I should have thought, quite your place . . .'

Traill sometimes dreamt early in the morning of French exercises, of the midday mutton, of Perrin's bony, ugly body watching the bath. If Traill had thought about it, he would have seen that Perrin did not like him.

The incident of the morning papers was equally trivial. Dormer always had breakfast in his own house, and that left therefore three of them. They clubbed together and provided three newspapers—the *Daily Mirror*, the *Daily Mail*, and a local affair. It was obvious that the person who came in last was left with the local paper. Perrin generally came in last, because he took early prep. in the Upper School, and he expected that the *Mirror* should be left for him. But Traill, as he paid the same subscription as Perrin, did not see why this should be. Clinton always took the *Daily Mail*, and therefore Perrin had to be contented with the *Western Morning News*. There was at last an argument. Traill refused to give way. The rest of the meal was eaten in absolute silence. Perrin came no more to Traill's room for an evening chat—a very small matter.

But at the end of the first month Traill did not see these things as in any way ominous. He could keep his boys in order. He liked his games of football; he was in a glow because he was in love—moreover, he had never quarrelled with any one in his life. He did not know whether he had made any progress with Isabel. It was very difficult to see her. She came down sometimes to watch them play football; after Chapel in the evening, he had walked up the little dark lane with her, the stars above the dark, cloudy trees, the leaves a carpet about their feet—and at every meeting he loved her more. When he had spare hours in the afternoon he liked to walk to the Brown Wood or down to the sea. Once or twice he bicycled over to Pendragon and had tea with the Trojans. Sir Henry Trojan was a man who had appealed to him greatly.

In spite of his size and strength and simplicity, his air of a man who lived out of doors and read little, he had a tremendous poetic passion for Cornwall. He showed Traill many things that were new to him. He began to feel a sense of colour; he saw the Brown Wood, the twisting, grey-roofed village, the sweeping, striving sea with fresh vision. He stopped sometimes in his walks and drew a deep breath at the way that the lights and colours were hung about him. Of course the contrast of his school life drove these other things against him—and also his love for Isabel.

These little things would have no importance were it not that they all helped to blind him to his true relations with Perrin. He did not think about Perrin at all; he did not think about his life even in any very definite way.

He never analysed things; he took things and used them.

And then at the end of that first month Birkland talked in the most amazing way. . . .

II

Traill had been attracted to Birkland from the first. The man had definite personality—aggressive in its influence—and contempt of the rest of the common room, but they justified it to some extent by their own terror of his tongue and their eager criticism of him behind his back.

He had treated Traill like the rest, but then

Traill never noticed it. He was not afraid of Birkland, he never resented his criticism, and he appreciated his humour.

And then suddenly one evening Birkland asked him to come and see him. His room was untidy—littered with school-books, exercise-books, many papers to be corrected; but behind this curtain of discomfort there were signs of other earlier things: some etchings, dusty and uncared for, sets of Meredith and Pater, some photographs, and a large engraving of Whistler's portrait of his mother. The latticed window was open, and from the night outside, blowing into the gusty candles, there were the scent of decaying leaves and a faint breath of the distant sea.

Birkland was thin—sticks of legs and arms; a short, wiry moustache; heavy, overhanging eyebrows; thin, straight, stiff hair turning a little grey. He gave Traill a drink, watched him fill a pipe; and then, huddled in his arm-chair, his legs crossed under him, his eyes full on the open window and the night sky, he asked Traill questions.

'And so you like it?'

'Yes—immensely!'

'Why?'

'Well—why not? After all, it gives a fellow what he wants. There's plenty of exercise—the hours are healthy—the fellows are quite nice fellows. I like teaching.'

Traill gave a sigh of satisfaction, and, after all, he had omitted his principal reason.

'Yes. How long do you mean to stay here?'

'Oh, a year, I suppose. Then I ought to get to Clifton.'

'Yes. You'd better not tell the Head that, though. How do you like the other men?'

'Oh, I think they're very good fellows. Dormer's splendid.'

'Yes—and Perrin?'

'Oh, he's all right. He seems to get annoyed pretty easily. As a matter of fact, I have felt rather irritated once or twice.'

'Yes — every one's wanted to cut Perrin's throat some time or other. As a matter of fact, I shouldn't wonder if it wasn't the other way round—one day.'

There was a pause, and then Birkland said, 'And so you like it?'

'Yes, of course; don't you?'

Birkland laughed. There was a long pause. Then Traill said again, rather uncertainly, 'Don't you?'

He had never thought of Birkland as an unhappy man—as a matter of fact, he never thought of people as being definite kinds of people, and he scarcely ever read novels.

Then Birkland spoke: 'You had better not ask me that, young man, if you want an encouraging answer.'

Then very slowly, after another pause, the words came out: 'I'm going to speak the truth to you to-night for the good and safety of your soul, and I haven't cared for the good and safety of any one's soul for—well!—I should be afraid to say how long. I'm afraid I don't really care very much about the safety of yours—but I care enough to speak to you; and the one thing I say to you is—get out—get away. Fly for your life.' His voice sank to a whisper. 'If you don't, you will die very soon—in a year perhaps. We are all dead here, and we died a great many years ago.'

Traill moved uncomfortably in his chair. He smiled across the flickering candles at Birkland.

'Oh, I say,' he said, 'that's a bit of exaggeration, isn't it? I suppose one is tired sometimes, of course; but, after all, there are a good many men in the country who make a pretty good thing out of mastering and aren't so very miserable.'

It was evident that he thought that it was all a kind of joke on Birkland's part. He pulled contentedly at his pipe.

But the other man went on: 'I shouldn't have said this at all if I hadn't meant it, and if I hadn't got twenty years of experience behind me to prove what I say. I don't know why I'm bothering you, I'm sure; but now I've begun I'm going on, and you've got to listen. You can't say you haven't been given your chance. Have you ever looked round the common room and seen what kind of men they are?'

'Of course,' said Traill; 'but,' he added modestly, 'I'm not observant, you know. I'm not at all a clever kind of chap.'

'Well, you would have seen what I'm telling you written in their faces right enough. Mind you—what I'm saying to you doesn't apply to the first-class public school. That's a different kind of thing altogether. I'm talking about places like Moffatt's—places that are trying to be what they are not—to do what they can't do—to get higher than they can reach. There are thousands of them all over the country—places where the men are underpaid, with no prospects, herded together, all of them hating each other, wanting, perhaps, towards the end of term, to cut each other's throats. Do you suppose that that is good for the boys they teach?'

He paused and relit his pipe, and his voice was, too, measured, but showing in its tensity his emotion.

'It's a different thing with the bigger places. There, there is more room; the men don't live so close together; they are paid better; there is a chance of getting a house; there is the *esprit de corps* of the school . . . but here, my God!'

Birkland bent forward, his face white, over the candles.

'Get out of it, Traill, you fool! You say, in a year's time. Don't I know that? Do you suppose that I meant to stay here for ever when I came? But one postpones moving. Another term will be better, or you try for a thing, fail, and get discouraged . . . and then suddenly you are too old—too old at thirty-three—earning two hundred a year . . . too old! and liable to be turned out with a week's notice if the Head doesn't like you—turned out with nothing to go to; and he knows that you are afraid of him and he has games with you.'

Traill stared at the little man's burning eyes. How odd of Birkland to talk like this!

'You think you will escape, but already the place has its fingers about you. You will be a different man at the end of the term. You will be allowed no friends here, only enemies. You think the rest of us like you. Well, for a moment perhaps, but only for a moment. Soon something will come . . . already you dislike Perrin. You must not be friends with the Head, because then we shall think you are spying on us. You must not be friends with us, because then the Head will hear of it and will immediately hate you because he will think that you are conspiring against him. You must not be friends with the boys, because then we shall all hate you and they will despise you. You will be quite alone. You think that you are going to teach with freshness and interest—you are full of eager plans, new ideas. Every plan, every idea, will be immediately killed. You must not have them—they are not good for examinations—you are trying to show that you are superior.'

Birkland paused. Traill moved uneasily in his chair.

'Wait! You must hear me out. It all goes

deeper than these things. It is murder—self-murder. You are going to kill—you have got to kill — every fine thought, every hope, that you possess. You will be laughed at for your ambitions, your desires. You will not even be allowed any fine vices. You must never go anywhere, because you are neglecting your work. You have no time. Here we are—fifteen men—all hating each other, loathing everything that the other man does—the way he eats, the way he moves, the way he teaches. We sleep next door to each other, we eat together, we meet all day until late at night—hating each other.'

'After all,' said Traill, still smiling, 'it is only a month or two, and there are holidays.'

'If term lasted another week or two,' went on Birkland quietly, 'murder would be committed. The holidays come, and you go out into the world to find that you are different from all other men—to find that they know that you are different. You are patronizing, narrow, egotistic. You realize it slowly; you see them shunning you—and then back you go again. God knows, they should not hate us—these others! they should pity us. If you marry, see what it is—look at Mrs. Dormer, Mrs. Comber, Mrs. Moy-Thompson. Look at their husbands, their life. There is marriage—no money, no prospects, perhaps at the end starvation! And gradually there creeps over you a dreadful and horrible inertia: you do not care—you do not think—you are a ghost. If one of us dies, we do not mind—we do not think about it. Only, towards the end of the term, when the examinations come, there creeps about the place a new devil. All our nerve is gone; our hatred of each other begins to be active. It is the end-of-termy devil. . . . Another week or two, and there is no knowing what we might do. We are all tired, horribly tired. Be careful then what you do and what you say.'

'My word!' said Traill, filling his pipe, 'what a horrible picture of things! You must be out of sorts. Why, it's hysteria!'

Birkland had crawled back into his chair again. He puffed at his pipe.

'Oh, of course you don't see it!' he said. 'After all, why should you? But it's true, every word of it. Oh, I'm resigned enough now. Besides, it's the beginning of the term. I'm inclined to think it's untrue, myself, just now. Wait and see. Watch White after he's had an interview with the Head—see Perrin and Comber together later on—study Mrs. Comber. But don't you bother. You won't listen to me—why should you? Only, in ten years' time you'll remember.'

After that they talked of other things. Birkland was rather amusing in his sharp, caustic way.

'I say,' said Traill as he stood by the door on the way out, 'that was all rot; wasn't it?'

'What was?' asked Birkland.

'Why, about the place—this place.'

'All rot!' said Birkland gravely.

III

But of course one dismisses these things very soon—especially, and immediately, if the person in question is Archie Traill.

Why think about a problematic and depressing future? Take these men that Birkland so gloomily points to as disappointing and unsatisfactory exceptions. Life is like that. There are always the riders who collapse into ditches and sit there mumbling, wishing for the company, down in the dirt and the grime, of their fellow-horsemen.

Meanwhile there is this fine autumn weather. Birkland remains a crabbed shadow; life is sharp, pungent—formed with faint blue skies, dim and shining like clear glass with a hard yellow sun stuck like a tethered balloon between saucer-clouds.

Archie Traill, on a free afternoon—an early frost had made the ground too hard for football—in the week after that Birkland evening, stood in the village street as the church clock struck half-past three, and he thanked God for a half-holiday.

The air was so still that the distant mining stamps and the breaking sea had it for the plain of their unceasing war, cannon against cannon, and the withdrawing rattle of their rival shot echoing against the blue horizon and the stiff side of the Brown Hill. The village cobbles shone and glittered; the grey roofs lay like carpets spread to dry. The brown church tower seemed to sway—so motionless was the rest of the world —with the clatter of its chiming clocks.

Suddenly Isabel Desart turned the corner. 'Good afternoon, Mr. Traill,' and the clasp of her hand was strong and clean as all the rest of her movements. She smiled at him as she always smiled, a little ironically and also a little seriously, as though she found the world a strange place, ought to think it a solemn one, but couldn't help finding it funny.

Three old women, their skirts kilted about them, their eyes fixed on vacancy, flung their voices into the silence like balls against a board.

'And she only sixteen—what a size!'

'Only sixteen—to think of it!'

'With her great legs and all!'

'Only sixteen . . .!'

The man and woman moved up the road together. She was usually so full of things to say that her silence surprised him. The thought that his presence could possibly be agitating to her, and therefore responsible, drove the blood to his head, and then he rebuked himself for a presumptuous fool. But if he had spoken, he would have had to tell her that he loved her—and it wasn't time yet.

But at last he broke against the silence very quietly. 'We must talk, one of us—it is so wonderfully quiet that it 's alarming.'

She turned round to him, and suddenly, so that he stopped in the road and looked at her, she put her hand on his arm.

'We are both so frightfully young,' she said.

'Why, yes,' he said, laughing at her; 'but why not?'

'Why, for the things that we 'll have to do. You for the boys, and I for my poor Mrs. Comber. I had thought when I saw you first that you were going to be old enough, but I don't think you are.'

'I know that I can't——' he began.

'Oh, it isn't for anything that you *can't* do!' she broke in. 'It 's just because you don't see it—why should you? You 're too much in the middle—I suppose it 's only outsiders who can really understand. But I get so depressed sometimes with it all that I think that I will leave it and go back to London and never come here again. One doesn't seem to be any use—no use at all. And it all seems worse in the autumn somehow. Poor Mr. Traill! I always happen to be gloomy when you catch me, and I 'm not gloomy really in the least.'

'But what is it all about? And don't go to London, please. You mustn't think of it.'

He was so much in earnest that she turned and looked at him. 'Why?' she said gravely. 'Do you like my being here?' And then, before he could say anything, she added, reflectively, 'Well, that 's one, at any rate.'

'I have to go in here,' she said, stopping before a gate with a drive behind it. 'Tea, you understand.' Then she gave him her hand. 'Although you don't in the least know what I mean, you 're a help,' she said; 'and I shall look across the chapel floor in the evening and know that I have a friend. Sometimes when I 'm down here—out of it—and everything 's so fresh and clear, like to-night, I think that it can't be true—the things that go on. Oh, I 'm so sorry for them, all of them!' She went through the gate and looked back at him. 'But I don't want to have to be sorry for you as well—please,' she added, and was lost in the trees.

But he, in his triumphant, buoyant sensation of things having moved a step—or even a good many steps further—was ready that she should be sorry or have any sensation whatever so long as she thought of him. Her claiming chapel-time as a meeting-ground made that somewhat irritating and so swiftly recurrent a ceremonial a thrice-blessed moment to which he might eagerly look forward throughout the day. But it is not my intention to give you all his symptoms—his passion is in no way the chief point; it was simply one of the things that helped in the culminating issue.

Isabel, meanwhile, found that throughout the tea-party her little conversation with Traill ran in her head. It was not a very interesting tea-party—three old ladies who regarded her as something very dangerous and alarming and offered her cake as though they expected it to turn into a bomb in her hands. She looked at their comfortable fire, their dark, cosy drawing-room, their caps and shawls, with the eye of someone whose passage through that country was very swift and whose language was not theirs. The dancing glow of the firelight, the tinkle of the tea-things, the softness of the rugs at her feet, were not the expression of her idea of life, and she flung them away from her and thought of Moffatt's and the night outside. Throughout their soft and courteous speech her mind was with Traill. He had said, 'Don't go to London, please,' and he had meant it—it was almost as though he had appealed to her from a sudden vision that he had of all that was in front of him. *She* knew, of course—she had seen it happen so very often before; and perceived that for this man, too, with his bright, eager challenge of life, his absurdly young notion of the way that things would be certain to be simple when they were never simple at all, grim, baffling disappointment was at hand. To her those red walls of Moffatt's were alive, moving—crushing, as in some story that she had once read, relentlessly the victims that were hidden within. Perhaps he had suddenly seen or understood something of that—there had come to him some forewarning. Her cheek reddened at the thought and her breath came quickly. She liked him—she had liked him from the first—she liked him very much; and if he wanted her to help him, she would do all that she could. She said good-bye to the three old ladies and, with a little humorous laugh, left them behind her. It was right that there should be three old ladies living like that, so cosily and comfortably, with their fires and their carpets, at the very foot of Moffatt's. How little people realized! These old ladies with their park gates and long drive! How they would roll up in their carriage! . . . and then Moffatt's!

It was dark, and the long hill that stretched above her was black and ominous. The lights of Moffatt's showed, to the right at the top, and the darker shape of its buildings cut the lighter grey of the sky. There was a lamp-post at the corner of the road, and as she closed the gates behind her with a clang she heard a voice say, 'Good evening, Miss Desart,' and saw that Mr. Perrin was at her side. Mr. Perrin always made her feel nervous, and now, in the dark, she instinctively shrank back, but it was only for an instant, and she was immediately ashamed of her fears. She could not see his face, but she fancied that his voice trembled—he seemed troubled about something; and then that feeling of pity that she had had for him before came upon her again, and her voice was softer and more tender.

'It was—um—a great piece of good fortune for me that I should be passing just when you were coming out—a great piece of good fortune.'

He seemed very nervous.

'And for me too,' she said; 'this hill grows extraordinarily dark, and I stayed on longer than

I ought to have done. Have you been paying calls, too?'

'Oh no! I—um—never pay calls—merely a stroll down to the village to buy some tobacco—merely that — nothing more . . . yes, merely that . . . simply some tobacco.'

She felt his agitation, and wished that the top of the hill might be reached as speedily as possible, but she fancied a little that he lingered. She hastened her steps.

'I 'm not sure that it isn't raining—I felt a drop just now, I thought—and it was such a lovely afternoon.'

'Oh no, I assure you——' and then he suddenly stopped.

She was frightened—quite unreasonably. She wanted to reach the warmth and light of Mrs. Comber's drawing-room as soon as possible and escape from this strange, awkward man.

She broke the silence. 'How is Mr. Traill getting on at the Lower School? I hope you all like him. The boys seem to have taken to him; but then, of course, his football is a quick road to favour.'

Mr. Perrin seemed to be swallowing his teeth. He coughed and choked. 'Ah, well, yes, Traill—young, of course, young, and one can only learn by experience. Perhaps just a little inclined to be cocksure—dangerous thing to be too certain—a fault of youth, of course.'

'Oh, I 've found him,' said Isabel, 'very modest

and pleasant. Of course I haven't seen very much of him, but I must say that what I 've seen of him I 've liked.'

They were nearly at the top of the hill; the big black gates cut the horizon.

In the light of the lamps at the corner of the road Isabel saw Mr. Perrin's face. It looked very white under the gaslight and he was clenching and unclenching his hands. His cap was on one side, his tie had risen at the back above his collar . . . his eyes were looking into hers and beseeching her like the eyes of a dumb animal.

They had come to the gates.

'Miss Desart . . .'

They both came to a halt in the road.

'Yes?' she said, smiling at him.

'I want you to . . . I 'd be awfully glad one day if . . .'

He stopped again desperately.

'What can I do?' she said, still smiling at him. He looked so odd, standing there in the dark, silent road . . . his hands restless. His eyes had moved from her face and were gazing up the road.

'I would be so glad if—one day—so flattered if —you would—will—um—come for a walk, one day.' He stopped with a jerk.

She moved through the gate and looked back at him before turning up the path to the house.

'Why, of course, Mr. Perrin, I shall be delighted. Good night.'

He stood looking after her.

CHAPTER V

A GAME OF FOOTBALL AND A DANCE IN PENDRAGON HAVE THEIR PART IN THE SCHEME OF THINGS

I

LATER there is Mr. Perrin heavily—with the mid-day mutton close about his head—surveying, in his dingy and tattered sitting-room, four small boys who gaze at him with staring eyes and jumping throats.

It is a piece of English poetry that has caught them, miserably, by the ears—Browning's *Patriot*, one verse a week, to be said every Tuesday morning first hour, and to be forgotten eagerly, completely forgotten, every Tuesday morning second hour.

'I go in the rain and, more than needs
The rope—the rope—the rope——'

Johnson Minor gazed miserably at his companions, and, finding no help in man, but only a jesting glory at his misfortunes, dizzily, despairingly, to the top row of Mr. Perrin's bookcase, where *Advanced Algebra* and *Mensuration* held perpetual war and rivalry.

It was a desperate affair altogether, because it was the afternoon of a football match—a great football match against a mighty Truro team—and already the gathering multitude in the field below flung a derisive murmur at the dusty panes.

But Mr. Perrin was motionless. He offered no assistance, he suggested no remedy, he merely tapped with his bone paper-knife on the red tablecloth—a tap that showed Johnson Minor once and for all that his case was hopeless:

'A rope—a rope that——'

Johnson Minor, with hanging head and red eyes, passed out to write it, the whole poem, fifty times before lock-up. He would miss the match. Outside, in the passage, he suddenly remembered the whole verse clearly, perfectly, but it was too late.

At last one prisoner only remained—Garden Minimus, a cheerful, untidy person aged ten, in enormous boots and no kind of parting to his hair.

Garden Minimus was the boy whom Perrin liked best in the whole school—had liked him best for the last two years. When things were really black, when headaches were violent, and when unpopularity seemed to hang about him in a dense, thick cloud, there was always Garden Minimus. He flattered himself that the boy was not aware of this partiality; but the boy, he was sure, liked him. He treated him always with an elaborate irony that the boy seemed to understand in some curious way. Garden would stand, with his head on one side like a rather intelligent small dog, and although he rarely said anything more than 'Yes, sir,' or 'No, sir,' Perrin felt that he grasped the situation.

On this afternoon it was plain that Garden Minimus did not know a word of *The Patriot,* and had made no attempt whatever to learn it.

Mr. Perrin looked at him with a slow smile. 'I 'm afraid, friend Garden,' he said, 'that it will devolve upon your lordship — hum — ha — that you should write this poem of the noble Mr. Robert Browning's no less than fifty times. I grieve—I sympathize—I am your humble servant; but the law commands.'

Garden Minimus brushed Mr. Perrin's fine periods aside, and said, with a most engaging smile, 'There 's a most ripping footer match this afternoon, sir.'

'Fool though I am,' said Mr. Perrin, 'I have nevertheless observed that there is, as you say, a footer match. Nevertheless, I am afraid *The Patriot* calls you, friend Garden.'

'It would be an awful pity,' said Garden reflectively, without paying the slightest attention to Mr. Perrin, 'to miss a decent game like that.'

Suddenly Mr. Perrin was irritated. He snapped out sharply, 'All right, Garden; that will do. You 'll get it a hundred times if you aren't careful!'

Garden, realizing his defeat, moved slowly out of the room, his forehead lowering. Outside the door he muttered, 'Silly, pompous ass!'

Mr. Perrin remained discontented, unhappy. He was continually attempting to make the boys fond of him and at the same time to retain his dignity. He never succeeded in this, because so definite an attempt on his part immediately precluded any capitulation on theirs. They thought he was a fool to try, and they resented his airs.

He was really fond of Garden Minimus, he thought, as he sat with his head between his arms in his dingy, dusty room. The dust wove patterns above his head in the pale, dim sunlight. He must go down and watch the football. He must get out amongst people, because he had a sickening fear that for the first time that term his headaches were coming back to him. He had avoided them. Miss Desart had been there instead, and every time that she spoke to him he had felt well and happy. She had spoken to him a good many times lately, and he now was sure that she was attracted to him. Soon he would ask her to go with him for a walk . . . then there would be more walks . . . then . . . He wrote to his mother that the thing was practically arranged.

As for that puppy, Traill—well, he'd kept him in his place, thank Heaven. As the days increased, Perrin had grown to dislike him more and more—conceited, insufferable, giving himself such airs. When he met any one who gave himself airs, Perrin had a curious habit of referring things back to his old mother and seeing her insulted. He could see the patronizing way that Traill would speak to her. This always made him furiously angry when he thought of it. But being furiously angry only brought on his headaches again. Oh, there were things to be done! He looked around his room and saw a pile of mathematical papers, some English essays. His eye crossed to the mantelpiece, and he saw there a silly china figure, painted in red and yellow, of an old gentleman in a cocked hat. This, for no reason that he could explain, always irritated him. The old gentleman had so confident and knowing a smile. He had always meant to get rid of it, but for some reason or other he never could destroy it.

Oh, he must get out into the air! His head was very bad.

As he left his room, there was a vague fear, somewhere, at his heart.

The game had begun. The ropes on either side were thickly lined with a dark crowd of boys, and a long wailing shout, 'Scho-o-l!' rose and fell without ceasing. Perrin, in his shabby great-coat, watched with a superior but interested air. There was nothing in the world that excited him more, but he had never been able to play himself, and so he affected to despise it.

In front of him, pressed against the ropes, were three small boys of his own house, each boy holding a paper bag from which he drew fat and sticky green and brown sweets. They had not noticed him. They divided their attention between their neighbours, their sweets, and the game.

'Shut up, Huggins, you silly fool! What are you shoving for?'

'Can't help it—Grey's barging—Oh, I say, run it, Morton! That's it! Pick it up—dodge him, man! Oh, hang it!'

'I say, swop one of those brown things for one of mine—Thanks! Where's Garden, you chaps?'

'Swotting up for Old Pompous.'

'Oh, what rot! I'm blowed if I would. I thought Pompous was rather sweet on Garden.'

'So he is—but Garden can't stand *him*.'

'No wonder—blithering ass, with his long words!'

'Oh, I say—they've got it! There's Morton off again—Oh, he's going! Well run, my word! He's in! No, he isn't! The back's got him! No, he hasn't! Hurray! Try! Good old Morton!'

Amongst the commotion that followed the happy event Perrin moved to a less crowded portion of the field. He was accustomed to hearing himself spoken of with but little respect by those who, when he was present, trembled before him. He always told himself that all the members of the staff were in the same box; but this afternoon it hurt—it hurt badly.

Little beasts! He'd punish them! As he moved along behind the ranks of boys—each boy with his friend—the familiar mantle of loneliness, that he had known so long, swept him in its sombre folds. He saw Comber in the distance, turned to avoid him, and suddenly confronted Mrs. Comber and Miss Desart.

He pulled himself up with a sudden effort of one who, feeling at his very worst, has immediately to appear at his very best, and the struggle was glaring to the observer, in the nervous clutching of the buttons of his coat and his uneasy, agitated laugh.

Mrs. Comber was always at her noisiest and most affable with Mr. Perrin, because she didn't like him, and she always tried to cover that dislike with an increased amiability. Isabel stood rather gravely by and watched the game.

'We appear to be winning,' said Perrin, glaring as he spoke at three small boys who had looked up at the sound of his voice. 'We appear—um—to be winning. Morton has secured a try.'

'Yes, I'm so glad,' gasped Mrs. Comber—she was out of breath. Morton's a nice boy—we had him once in our house, and I do hope the school will win, because it's so nice for everybody's tempers, and the boys like it—and there's that nice Mr. Traill playing and running about most beautifully.'

Perrin started. He hadn't noticed that Traill was playing. He looked at Isabel and saw that she was watching the game with deep attention. Traill was certainly in his element. The ball came suddenly in his direction. He had it in his hands and was off with it. There was a breathless, hushed pause; then, as he sped along, just inside the touch-line, swerved past his opposing three-quarter to the centre of the field, and flew for the goal, the silence broke into a roar. Miss Desart gave a long-drawn 'Oh!' Mrs. Comber a little scream, Mr. Perrin moodily stroked his moustache.

The back was outwitted, and came floundering to the ground—a very pretty try.

'Good old Traillers!' 'That's something like!' 'Isn't he spiffing?'—and then Miss Desart's 'Oh, that was splendid!' beat about Mr. Perrin's poor head, that was aching horribly.

'That nice Mr. Traill! I do like to see people run like that. Oh, it's half-time.'

Mrs. Comber caught Mr. Perrin slowly into her vision again and prepared once more to be volubly pleasant.

But Mr. Perrin had had enough. On the opposite side of the field, on the top of the hill against the china white of the autumn sky, were three trees, gnarled, bent, gaunt, like three old men. Quite alone they stood and watched, impersonally and gravely, the game. Mr. Perrin felt suddenly as though he, too, were really one of them. Behind them sheets of white light, falling from the hidden sun, flooded the long, brown fields.

Cold pale blue was reflected against the grey stodgy clouds. Mr. Perrin went back slowly to his room. The dusty untidiness of it closed about him. He sat down to his pile of English essays on 'Town and Country—Which is the best to live in?' with a confused sense of running men, lights across the hills, the china red and black man on the mantelpiece, and Miss Desart's shining eyes.

At five o'clock, with a heavy scowl, Garden Minimus presented *The Patriot* neatly written fifty times.

II

It was about this time that Archie Traill accepted an invitation to a dance at Sir Henry Trojan's. It was to be only a small dance, and it was to be over by twelve. 'Do let us,' Lady Trojan wrote, 'put you up. You will be able to see more of Robin, who is coming down for the night from London. He will want to see you so badly.' Traill wrote back, accepting the dance, but explaining that he must return on the same evening, quoting as his imperative necessity early morning preparation.

It was Clinton's evening on duty, and therefore there was no very obvious necessity to say anything more about it; but Traill, in order to free himself from any further danger, thought that he would go and receive definite permission from Moy-Thompson. He had not as yet been to a single dinner or evening party outside the school, and he had noticed that the rest of the staff never went out at all, nor had apparently any intention of doing so. He went round at twelve o'clock after morning school to Moy-Thompson's study, knocked on the door, and entered. He was conscious at once of trouble in the air. He saw that White, the nervous man who took the Classical Fifth, was standing by Thompson's table. He moved back as though he would leave the room; but the head master called to him, 'Ah! Traill, don't go. I shall be ready in a moment.'

Then Traill noticed several things. He noticed, first, that Moy-Thompson's garden beyond the window was coloured a brilliant brown in the sun; he noticed that Moy-Thompson's study was dark and black, like a prison; he noticed that White's long hatchet-face was yellow in the half-light; he noticed that both White's hands, hanging straight at his side, were tightly clenched, and that his thin legs, spread widely apart, were drawn stiffly beneath his trousers so that the cloth flapped a little against his thin calves; he noticed that Moy-Thompson's long grey beard swept the table and that his fingers tapped the wood every now and again with the sound of peas rattling on a plate; he noticed that Moy-Thompson was smiling.

Moy-Thompson said, 'But I think I told you that Maurice was on no account to have an exeat.'

White's voice came from a far, hesitating distance: 'Yes, I know. But his father was only to be in London for an hour, and he has not seen his son for a year, and I thought that under the circumstances——'

'That does not alter the fact that I had expressed a wish that he should not have an exeat.'

'No—but I thought that if you knew all the circumstances of the case, you would not object.'

'What is your position here? Are you here to consider my wishes? What are you paid to do?'

White made no answer.

'Of course if you are dissatisfied with the condition of things here, you have only to say so. It would be doubtless possible to fill your place.'

'No,'—White's voice was very low—'I have no complaint. I am sorry if——'

'You must remember your position here. I have yet to discover any paid position that enables you to indulge your own particular fancies when you please. Doubtless you are better informed.'

Traill could endure it no longer. He was so angry that the blood had rushed to his head, and his face was scarlet. White had flung one glance at him, as though to beseech him to go away, and he moved to the door; but again Moy-Thompson said, 'Just a moment, Traill.'

He was so angry that, on the impulse of the moment, he had almost stepped across the room and flung in his resignation. White's long haggard figure was torture; it was cruelty, devilish cruelty, laughing with them there in the room.

The man at the table was playing with them as a cat does with a mouse, shaming one of them before the younger man, as though he had stripped him naked and driven him so into the playing-fields outside, forcing the other to listen, brutally, intolerably, against his will.

The room seemed full of pain—it seemed to cross and recross in waves. White's head bent down. . . . At last he passed with lowered eyes out through the door.

Traill could not speak; without another word, he turned and followed him. Outside the door in the darkened passage he suddenly held out his hand and caught White's. White held his for an instant; suddenly, with a frightened, startled look, he slipped away.

III

When the evening of the dance arrived, Traill noticed that he was glad to get away. Term had now lasted for six weeks, and in another week it would be half-term. He was a little tired; he found it more difficult to get up in the morning. Little things mattered a great deal—he now emphatically disliked Perrin more than he had ever disliked any one in his life before; there was even annoyance in the mere sight of his long, lean, untidy figure, in the sound of his assured, supercilious voice, in the sense of his arrogance.

They never spoke to each other if they could help it; meals were extremely disagreeable.

He found, too, that love did not mingle properly with school work. He was always going into daydreams when he should have been teaching his form. He tried to keep the sea and the wood and the funny man that he had met there and

Isabel apart from his work; but they came skipping in—and at night he dreamt—he was almost sure that she loved him. . . . Whenever they met now they were very silent.

He escaped whilst they were all in chapel. He lit his bicycle-lamp, wrapped a long, thin coat about him, and escaped. It had been a cold, fine day. The sun was just setting over the sea as he spun down the hard, white road.

As he flew between the dark, sweet-scented hedges, as he felt the wind in his ears and about his face, as the smell, salt and sharp, of the sea came to him, it was strange to find how the cares and troubles of those brown buildings on the hill fled away from him. He was already his old self; he sang to himself.

A faint red glow hovered over the dark, heaving water; the trees stood black on the horizon, and the long, low lines of shadow, white and grey, stole about the road as the evening sky slowly settled, with a little sighing of the wind, into the colours that it would bear during the night. The lights of the little village behind him made a red cluster against the dark shoulder of the Brown Hill.

He sang aloud.

It was a most enjoyable dance; he had never enjoyed a dance so much before. He realized that he was looking on the past six weeks as imprisonment; he also noticed that when he told his partners that he was a schoolmaster they stared at him a little apprehensively. It was delightful to see Robin Trojan again. They walked into the garden and strolled about the paths together; he was much improved since the Cambridge days, Traill thought—less self-assured and with wider interests. And then Sir Henry Trojan always gave Traill a broader feeling of life—sanity and health and strength—and he had an admirable sense of humour.

And then it was over, and Traill was speeding back over the hill again. He thought of Isabel all the way back. He fancied that she was with him in the dark. The night was so black that he could see only the little round white circle that his lamp flung on the road in front of him. The hedges, like black, bulging pillows, closed him in.

He seemed to be back in no time. He heard the school clock strike one. He took the Yale key and fitted it into the door; it would not move; he tugged, pulled it out, forced it in again, and pushed it. With a click it broke in half.

He looked at the big, black, silent buildings in despair—supposing he had to stay out all night? He would die rather than ring.

He went round to the other side of the building and looked up. Then he saw that the dining-room windows were not very high and that he might climb. He caught on to a buttress and pulled himself up; then another hand on the window-sill drew him level.

He found to his delight that the window was

not latched. He pushed it up, and then with one hasty look into the dark cavern beneath him, jumped. He was saluted on his descent with a noise as though all the crockery in the world had fallen about his ears. The sharp collapse of it seemed to go rushing through the silent house for hours; he knew that he had cut his hand and had bruised his knee.

For a moment he was stunned; then slowly he realized what he had done: the tables were laid for the next morning's breakfast, and he had jumped down straight amongst the cups and plates.

He sat up on the floor and began, with his head aching, to stanch the blood that came from the cut. He saw, as in a dream, the door open. Someone was standing there in a nightshirt holding a candle; it was Perrin.

'Who 's there? What 's that?' Perrin held a poker in his other hand.

Traill got up slowly from the floor. 'It is I—Traill,' he stammered. He was still feeling stunned.

Perrin held the candle a little closer. 'Oh, is it you, Traill?'

'Yes, I have been out. I fell on to the plates and things. I am sorry.'

'You made a great noise.' Perrin was speaking very slowly. 'You woke me up.'

'Yes; I am most awfully sorry.'

Traill moved towards the door. Perrin still stood there, holding his candle, his nightshirt flapping about his legs. He did not seem inclined to move.

'You made a great noise. It is one o'clock.' He said it as though he were Robespierre condemning Louis XVI to execution.

'Yes, I know. I 'm dreadfully sorry. I broke my key.'

Still Perrin did not move. 'What are you doing out so late?' he said at last, slowly.

What the devil had it to do with Perrin!

'I didn't know that this was a girls' school,' Traill said at last sarcastically. His head was aching, his knee hurt, he was tired, and in a very bad temper.

Perrin moved from the door. 'It 's struck one—coming in like this!'

The candle flung a most ridiculous shadow of him on the wall—a huge, gigantic head with hair sticking out of it like spears.

Because he was tired and rather hysterical, this suddenly amused Traill enormously. He burst into a peal of laughter.

'I can't help it,' he said, shaking; 'you look so funny, so frightfully odd!'

Perrin said nothing. He looked at him for a moment. He had been disturbed in his sleep; he had every reason to be very angry. But he said nothing at all. He moved slowly down the passage.

Traill followed him in silence; he was suddenly frightened.

CHAPTER VI

SAEVA INDIGNATIO

I

To Perrin, in his sleep that night, there came, accompanied with roaring wind and crashing sea, a dream of the little man in red and black china that lived on the mantelpiece. He came tip-tap across the floor to him and bent over the bed and whispered in his ear. He had grown in his transit and was large in the leg and trailed behind him a long black gown, and he troubled Mr. Perrin by buzzing like a wasp.

He was urging Perrin to do something, but it was hard to distinguish the words because of the booming of the sea. The cold light of early morning, and an hour later, the harsh clang of the bell down the stone passages, restored the china gentleman once more to the mantelpiece; but the discovery that there had been a storm in the night only seemed to confirm the gentleman's appearance. Besides, he was no new thing—he had climbed down from his perch on other occasions.

Perrin and Traill exchanged no word during breakfast.

II

Garden Minimus played his small part in the whole affair by being sulky and obstinate during the whole of first hour. It was a game that he was perfectly accustomed to playing, and he knew every move from the opening gambit of 'saying things under your breath that looked bad, but couldn't possibly be heard,' to the triumphant checkmate of a studied, sarcastic politeness that was most unusual and hinted at danger.

Perrin had slept, as we have seen, exceedingly badly, and the old hallucination that twenty boys were in reality five hundred crept over him. They sat in stupid, irritated rows at hard wooden desks soiled with ink. Beyond the drab windows the wind howled, and the dry leaves blew against the panes.

His temper rose as the hour advanced. The fifth proposition of the first book of Euclid was scarcely calculated to show dull boys at their brightest and best, and Perrin found, by changing the letters of the figure on the board, that the form knew nothing about it at all.

He proceeded, as was his way, to secure the dullest, fattest, and heaviest boy (a youngster with spectacles and a protruding chin, called Pomfret-Walpole) and to make merry at his expense. Pomfret-Walpole—his fingers exuded ink, his coat whitewash, and his hair dust—stood with his mouth open and his brow wrinkled, and a vague wonder as to why, when he ought to be thinking about Euclid, his mind would invariably wander to the bristly hairs at the back of Mr. Perrin's neck and the silly leaves dancing about outside.

Mr. Perrin played heavily with him for about a quarter of an hour (the form laughing nervously at his ironical sallies), and then sent the youngster back, crying, to his seat; the boy spent the rest of the hour in drawing hideous people with noses like pens and tiny legs, and then smudging them out with his fingers.

Then Perrin had Garden Minimus in his hands. The boy's sulking, frowning face drove him to fury. He suddenly felt (as though it had leapt wildly from some dark corner on to his shoulder) the Cat of Cruelty purring at his ear. It was an animal whose whispers he heard, as a rule, only when the term was well advanced; now it was upon him. He knew, suddenly, that he would like to take Garden Minimus's ears in his hands and twist them back further and further until they cracked. He would like to take his little fat arms and close his fingers about them and pinch them until they were blue. He would like to take the sharp, white knuckles and beat them with a ruler. Garden had chubby cheeks and bright blue eyes. Perrin began to pull, very gently, his hair. Garden wriggled a little.

'Take the triangle A B C,' he began, and

stopped. Perrin began to pinch the back of his neck.

'You have said that six times now, Garden. Say it again, because I am sure the rest of the form are immensely interested. Really, I grieve to think of the amount of time that you must have spent over your preparation last night. You 'll be overdoing it if you go on like this, you know—you will, really. You mustn't work so hard. Meanwhile write it out thirty times, and say it to me to-night after tea.'

But he did not let him go. He passed his hand down the boy's arm. . . . He saw the form watching him with white faces; his own was white; he was shaking with rage.

'Go back to your seat,' he said in a whisper, and he gave him a push. He sent the form back to learn the work again, and he sat for the rest of the hour with his head between his hands. Then, when the bell had rung and most of the form had filed out, he called Garden to him. 'I think fifteen times will be enough,' and he touched the boy's sleeve with his hand. But Garden went out of the room in silence, infinite contempt in his eyes.

Then, the boys gone, Mr. Perrin's mind went back to the incident of the preceding night. It was his custom to go and talk for a little to Moy-Thompson once a week. They disliked each other, of course; but they could be of mutual advantage, and they both found that hints dropped and accepted during these little talks were of great value during the days that followed. Perrin had never any deliberate intention of harming any one in these little conversations. But, every man's hand being against him, it seemed to him only fair that he should use such opportunities of retaliation as were given him. At the same time these little confidential talks flattered his sense of power. Dormer was the senior master at the Lower School, but Perrin knew that Dormer did not have these little talks; it did not occur to him that the reason might be that Dormer was too honourable to care about them. Moreover, so far as Traill was concerned, Perrin really felt that it did not do to have masters leaping through windows at any hour of the night. The accidental fact that he disliked Traill intensely had, he persuaded himself, nothing whatever to do with it; he would have felt it just as strongly his duty to speak about it had the offender been his dearest friend.

The accumulative irritations of the morning, succeeding a disturbed and broken night, only stirred him to further zeal for the school's good. The only consoling fact in a dark world was that Miss Desart had, in chapel, last evening, looked at him with eyes that seemed to him on fire with devotion. He intended, in a day or two, to ask her to come for a walk with him . . . and then another walk . . . and then another . . . and then . . .

And so he went to see Moy-Thompson. You

can, if the simile is not too terribly old, imagine Moy-Thompson as a spider and his study as his web; it was certainly dusty enough, with faded busts of Romans and Greeks on the top shelves of the bookcases, and gloomy photographs of gloomy places on the walls. The two men seemed to suit the place well enough, and its depression really brightened Mr. Perrin up. But it must be remarked once more that it was not from any anticipation of doing Traill damage that he embraced and cuddled his little piece of news so eagerly, but only because it helped his sense of importance. He was already wishing that he had told Garden Minimus to write his Euclid thirty times instead of fifteen, so cheered and inspirited did he feel.

The two men understood one another perfectly, and had a mutual respect for each other's strong qualities. No time was wasted in preliminaries, and it was a curious coincidence that Moy-Thompson's first question should be: 'What do you think of Traill? How 's he doing?'

Moy-Thompson is not a pleasant person to contemplate; alone, amongst the people of that place, there is nothing whatever to be said for him, and it is my intention to pass over him as quickly as may be. Perrin knew from the sound of his voice that he had some reason for disliking Traill.

'Oh, I think, well enough,' he answered, looking out of the window. 'The boys like him.'

'Oh, they like him, do they?'

'Yes. I think he indulges them rather. I'm not quite sure that he sticks to his work as he should do.'

'Why! What does he do?'

'I found him jumping through the Lower School dining-room window at one o'clock this morning.'

'Oh, did you!' Moy-Thompson smiled. 'Where had he been?'

'I didn't ask.'

Perrin pulled his gown about him. A sudden distaste for the whole business had seized him; after another word or two he went away, back to his own rooms.

III

Meanwhile Traill was tired and cross and out of temper with the world. He found that there was more to be said for the stay-at-home tastes of the rest of the staff than he had suspected. You couldn't, if you went gaily dancing the evening before, embrace early morning preparation with the eagerness and even the attention that it properly demanded. His mind was heavy, drowsy; he had forgotten his anger with Perrin and was only rather amused by the whole affair of the night before; but, instead of correcting Latin exercises, he sat, with his eyes gazing dreamily out of the window, his thoughts on Isabel.

He found first hour tiresome and irritating. He lost his temper for the first time that term, and went, at the end of the second hour, into the Upper School common room with a cloudy brow and dragging feet.

Anything drearier than this place it would be impossible to conceive. There was a long, red-clothed table, a black, yawning grate, a dozen stiff wooden chairs and, scattered about the room, the whole staff waiting for the bell to ring for third hour. This was the most irritating quarter of an hour of the day.

Several men, Comber, Clinton, Dormer, and another, were bending over the table, supervising the selection of the team for the afternoon's match. As Traill came in he heard Comber's voice: 'Toggett at three-quarter is perfectly absurd. That's obviously Traill's choice. Traill may be able to play himself, but his knowledge of the theory of the game is absolutely nil.' Comber had resented Traill's entrance into the school football from the very first. He, although many years past his game, had hitherto led the Rugby enthusiasts of the school—he had been supreme on the Committee and had had the last word about the teams. Traill's football, however, was so obviously superior to anything that the school had had for a great many years that he was received with open arms. He had not perhaps been as judiciously submissive to Comber as he might have been, but he had always deferred to his opinion and had never been goaded by Comber's caustic contradictions into ill-temper.

He did not now show any ill-temper, but only, with a laugh as he came up to the table, said, 'Thanks, Comber.'

Dormer hurried to make peace, but Comber continued to mutter: 'What the devil you want to put the man there for, I can't think. . . .'

By the window Birkland and Monsieur Pons were arguing about the latter's discipline.

'I should get them to stamp and rush about a bit more, Pons, if I were you,' Birkland was saying. 'It's so delightful for me, being just under you. It is so easy for me to do my work, so nice to think that they really *are* enjoying themselves.'

Monsieur Pons was waving his arms excitedly. 'I keep them perfectly still this morning, as still as one mouse. No one stirs. You can hear a pin drop.'

'You must have dropped a cartload of them,' said Birkland, frowning. 'Try and drop less next time.'

Suddenly in the middle of the room there appeared the school sergeant. That could only mean one thing, and conversation instantly ceased.

'Mr. Moy-Thompson wishes to see Mr. Traill at twelve,' he said.

Comber gave a grunt of satisfaction. Traill laughed. 'I thought things were a little too pleasant to last,' he said. His mind flew back to the incidents of last night. Surely Perrin couldn't have said anything! Probably Moy-Thompson had heard of it in some other way. He shrugged his shoulders and thought, as he looked round the dreary room, that schoolmastering wasn't always pleasant. He wondered, too, a little unhappily, why, when one wanted things to go well, everything should go wrong, through no fault of one's own.

Here were Perrin and Comber, for instance; they both obviously disliked him, and yet he had done nothing to either of them. As he went out, he caught White looking at him timidly, but sympathetically, and he smiled at him. And indeed at twelve, when he knocked on the door at the end of the dark passage, it was chiefly his memory of the last occasion that he had been there, of White's pale face, that remained with him.

Pathos has, too, often its intense, pathetic moment, coming, for no definite reason, out of a mysterious distance and choosing to fill, as water fills a pool, rooms and places and companies of people. Now, suddenly, this study with Moy-Thompson in it was a place, to Traill, of the intensest pathos, so that it seemed strange that, with such brilliant things as the world contained, it should be allowed to continue. His own position was lost in the perpetual vision of White standing, as he had seen him, with bent head.

'Ah, Traill,' said Moy-Thompson. 'Sit down. I have been wanting to have a talk with you. I hope that this time is quite convenient?'

'Perfectly,' said Traill.

'I've been intending to come down and look at your form, but I have had no opportunity. I must try and manage next week.'

Traill said nothing. Moy-Thompson smiled at him. 'I hope that you have had no trouble with discipline.'

'None. The boys are excellent.'

'Ah! that is splendid.' There was a pause; then the beard was suddenly lifted, and a glance was flashed across the table. 'I hope that you take your work seriously, Mr. Traill.'

Traill flushed a little. 'I think that I do,' he said.

'That is well. . . . Because we are—ah! um—a great institution, a very great institution. We owe our traditions—um, eh—a very serious and determined attention to detail. To work together, as one man, for the good of our race, that must be our object. Yes. No divisions, all in friendly brotherhood—um, yes.'

Traill said nothing.

'I hope you realize this. We want every energy, every nerve, at work. We must not waste a moment, nor grudge every instant to the cause we have at heart. Um, yes, I hope that you agree, Mr. Traill.'

'I hope,' Traill said, 'that you have not found

me wanting, that you have nothing to complain of. I think that I have worked——'

'Worked? Ah, yes.' Moy-Thompson caught him up, cracking his fingers together. 'But what about play, eh? What about play?'

Traill flushed. 'As to football——'

'No, it is not football. It is merely a detail—quite a detail. But Mr. Perrin informs me that you came in at one o'clock this morning through the window. I confess that I was surprised.'

'That is quite true,' said Traill, in a low voice. 'I went——'

'Ah! no! please!' Mr. Thompson lifted a large white hand. 'No details are necessary. The facts are sufficient. I need not, I think, say any more. You must see for yourself. . . . Only, I think you will agree with me that it should not occur again.'

'I am sorry——' said Traill.

'Ah, please! No more; it shall not be mentioned again. Only, work and play together are impossible. We have long vacations that give us all we ask. To pass for a moment to another matter.' Moy-Thompson put his hand on some papers. 'Here are the scholarship questions that you have set—geography and history. I think they are scarcely what we require. If you would not mind resetting them and bringing them to me to-morrow. Yes. Thank you. . . . Good morning.'

Traill rose, took the papers in his hand, and

left the room. He knew, surely, certainly, as though Birkland himself had told him, that this was to be the beginning of persecution. The Reverend Moy-Thompson had got his knife into him, and he had Perrin to thank for it.

IV

The interview that had lasted barely five minutes hung heavily over him throughout the midday dinner. He always hated the meal: the great joints of mutton waiting to be carved, in shapeless, thick hunks, the incessant noise throughout the meal, the clatter of plates and noise and voices, the dreary monotony and repetition of it—Perrin's face seen at the end of a long white table with the two rows of boys in between.

But to-day as he sat there he felt that he could kill Perrin if he had the opportunity. What business was it of his? He had at any rate lost no time in running to tell Moy-Thompson about it. The thought of the savage joy that must have filled Perrin's breast whilst he told his news made Traill grind his teeth. Well, he would be even with him!

The moment the meal was over, and grace had been chanted in a loud, discordant yell, Traill left the table and, without a word to any one, rushed down to the sea.

A tremendous wind was blowing. There was a certain part of the cliff that jutted out into the water, and this was surrounded now, on three sides, by a furious, heaving flood.

Wet mist hung over the sea, so that the enormous breakers leapt out of the sea, came whistling with a thousand arms into the sky, and then fell with a deafening roar upon the rocks. One after another, in swift succession, first suspended in mid-air, hanging there like serpents about to strike, then falling in a curve with glistering, shining backs, sweeping, tearing, at last lashing the iron rock. About him the wind screamed and tugged at his clothes; behind him the trees bent and creaked along the road; the rain lashed his face.

He was seized with a kind of fury; he stood, facing the sea, with his hands clenched, his head up, his cap in his hand, and Isabel Desart, as she came battling down the road and saw him there, knew, in that moment, that she loved him and had loved him from the first moment that she saw him. He saw her, but they could not speak to one another; the noise was too great—the waves, the wind, the bending trees caught them into their clamour; they stood, side by side, in silence. Suddenly he put out his hand and caught hers. He held it; still, without a word, with the wind almost flinging them to the ground, they drew together. The mist swept about their heads, the spray beat in their faces. He drew her closer to him, and she yielded. For a moment he held her with his face pressed close against hers, and then their lips met. At last, and still without a word, they moved slowly down the road. . . .

V

It was about half-past nine when Perrin, looking up at the sound of the opening door, saw Traill standing there. Traill filled the doorway, and Perrin knew at once that there was going to be a disturbance. He had had disturbances before, a good many of them, and always it had brought to him a sense of pathos that he, with an old mother (he always saw her as a crumpled but vehement background), should have always to be fighting people—he, so unoffending if they would let him alone. However, if any one (especially Traill) wished to fight him, he would do his best.

Traill was frowning. Traill was very angry.

Perrin said, 'Ah, Traill! Come in for a chat? That 's good of you. Splendid! Sit down, won't you? Anything I can do for you?' But he wasn't smiling.

'No,' said Traill slowly. 'There 's nothing you can do for me. But I want to speak to you.'

'Ah, well, sit down, won't you?'

'No, thanks. I 'll stand.' Traill cleared his throat. 'Did you by any chance say anything to the Head about my coming in last night?'

Perrin smiled. 'My dear Traill, I really can't remember; and is it really, after all, any business of yours?'

'Only this much, that he has been speaking to me about it. He says that you told him—I want to know why you told him.'

'It is my business,' Perrin said, 'as house-master here to find out anything that may be harming my house. I consider your late hours, your disregard of your work, prejudicial to the school's progress—um, yes.'

The impulse that had brought Traill to Perrin's room had not altogether been one of anger. He was much too excited by the other event of the afternoon to have any very angry feelings against any one, and indeed it had been rather a desire for peace, for clearing things up and being well with the world, that had brought him there. He was a little ashamed of the way that he had allowed, during these last weeks, his anger against Perrin to grow, and he seemed to be losing some of his good-humour and equability.

So now he put all the self-command that he possessed into play, and said quietly, 'I 'm sorry, Perrin, if you feel that I have been neglecting my duty. I don't think that, after all, one night's outing during the term can do any one very great harm. But I only spoke to you about it because I have been feeling during these last weeks that we have not been very good friends. It seems a pity when we are cooped up together here so closely that we should not get on as well as possible; it makes everything uncomfortable. And, in so far as I am to blame at all, I am very sorry.'

The little red and yellow china man on the mantelpiece, Perrin saw, had been watching the conversation with great curiosity, and Perrin felt that he was a little disappointed now when matters promised to finish comfortably. Perrin himself was only too ready for peace. These quarrels always brought on headaches, and, in his heart, he longed eagerly, hungrily, for a friend. He already was beginning to feel again that he liked young Traill very much.

He sat back in his chair and meant to be pleasant once more; but it was his eternal misfortune, his curse from the deriding gods, that he had ever at his back the memory of all these jesting years that had already passed him by: the memory of the men, the boys, the women, who had laughed at him: the memory of the ways that he had suffered, of the taunting jeers that had been flung at him, of the jests that so many of his fellow-beings had, in his time, played upon him.

And so now he felt that at all costs he must regain his dignity, he must show this young fellow his place and then be nice to him afterwards; and really, somewhere in the back of his mind, he saw his old mother with her lace cap sitting stiffly in her chair, and Traill on his knees, kissing her hand.

'Well, Traill, I 'm sure I 'm glad you feel like that—um, yes. One must, you know, maintain discipline. You are young; when you are older, you will see that there is something in what I say—um. We know, you see; schoolmastering is a thing that takes some learning; yes, well, I 'm sure I 'm very glad.'

But Traill was white again; his good determinations, his pleasant tempers were flung, suddenly screaming, helter-skelter to the winds. The patronage of it, the stupid, blundering fool with his 'When you are older,' and the rest!

'All right,' he said hotly; 'keep that advice for others. I don't know that I was so wrong, after all. What business of yours was it to go sneaking to the Head like that? There are certain things that a gentleman doesn't do.'

'Oh, really!'—the little man on the mantelpiece was smiling again. Perrin was snarling, and his hands gripped the sides of his chair. 'Your apologies seem a little premature. One can forgive something to your age, but that sort of impertinence—— I don't think you remember to whom you are speaking. You are the junior master here, you must be taught that, and when those who are wiser than yourself choose to give you some advice, you should take it gratefully.'

Traill took a step down the room, his hands clenched.

'My God! you conceited, insufferable——'

'Get out of my room!'

'All right, when I 've told you what I 've thought of you.'

'Get out of my room!' Perrin's eyes were starting out of his head.

Traill swung on his heel. 'I won't forget this in a hurry,' he said.

'Take care you don't come in here again,' Perrin shouted after him. The door was banged.

Perrin sat back in his chair; the room was going round and round, and he had a confused idea that people were running races. He pressed his hands to his head; the little china man leapt, screaming, off the mantelpiece and ran at him, kicking up his fat little legs; and with the breeze from under the door, a pile of French exercises fluttered, blew like sails in the wind, and then slid, scattering, to the floor.

CHAPTER VII

THE BATTLE OF THE UMBRELLA: THEY OPEN FIRE

I

BUT, during the week that followed, Traill's good-temper slowly reasserted itself once more. After all, it was really impossible to be angry with any one when the world was alight and trembling with so wonderful an adventure. They had each of them written to those in authority. Isabel had a complacent father who knew something of young Traill's family and, answering at once, said that he would come down to see them and made it his only stipulation that the engagement should last for at least a year, until they were both a little older. Traill's mother was delighted with anything that could give her son such happiness. It had all been very sudden of course; but then, was not true love always like that? Had not she, a great many years ago, fallen in love with Archie's father 'all in a minute,' and was not that the beautiful incautious way that the new practical generation seemed so often to forget? So, she sent him her blessing and also wrote a little note to Isabel.

But they still kept their secret from the others. They meant every day to reveal it, but they shrank, as each morning came, from all the talk and chatter that would at once follow. It would mean an end, Isabel knew, to any easy and pleasant relations that she might have with any one at the school. She never understood the reason, but she knew that they would feel that she had acted in a conceited, presuming manner. It would not be pleasant.

So their meetings were, during these days, few and difficult. They met in the wood and at the sea, and their eyes crossed over the chapel floor, and they even wrote to one another and posted their letters elaborately in the letter-box.

But on any morning the secret might be revealed. Traill told Isabel about his quarrel with Perrin, and she urged him to make it up.

'When we ourselves are so happy,' she said, 'we can't quarrel with any one—and, poor man, no wonder his temper is irritable. He 's a miserably disappointed man, and I don't think he 's very well either. He looks dreadfully white and strained sometimes. We can afford to put up with some ill-temper from other people, Archie, just now. When we are so happy and he is so unhappy, it is a little unfair, isn't it?'

And so he kissed her and went back resolved to be pleasant and agreeable. But Perrin gave him no opportunity. They spoke to each other a little at meals for appearance' sake, but any advances that Traill made were cut short at once without hesitation.

Perrin passed about the passages and the class-rooms during this week heavily, with a white face and a lowering brow—he had headaches, bad headaches; and his form suffered.

II

And so it was suddenly, without warning or preparation, that the storm broke—the storm that was to be remembered for years afterwards at Moffatt's: the great Battle of the Umbrella, about which strange myths grew up, that will become, doubtless, in later centuries at Moffatt's a strange Titanic contest, with gods for its warriors and thunderbolts for their weapons: the great battle that involved not only the central combatants, not only Traill and Perrin and their lives and fortunes, but also others—the Combers, the matrons, the masters, the whole world of that place seized by the Furies . . . and, in the corner, in that umbrella-stand by the hall door, underneath the stairs, that faded green umbrella—now, we suppose, passed into that limbo into which all umbrellas must eventually go, but then the gage, the glove, the sign token of all that was to come.

Let, moreover, no one imagine that these things are not possible. This Battle of the Umbrella stands for more, for far more, than its immediate contest. Here is the whole protest and appeal of all those crowded, stifled souls buried of their own original free will beneath fantastic piles of scribbled paper, cursing their fate, but unable to escape from it, seeing their old age as a broken, hurried scrambling to a no-man's grave, with no dignity nor suavity, with no temper nor discipline, with nerves jangling like the broken wires of a shattered harp—so that there is no comfort or hope in the future, nothing but disappointment and insult in the past, and the dry, bitter knowledge of failure in the present—this is the Battle of the Umbrella.

It was Monday morning, and Monday morning is worse than any other day of the week.

There has been, in spite of many services and the reiteration of religious stories concerning which a shower of inconvenient questions are flung at the uncertain convictions of authority, a relief in the rest and repose of the preceding day.

Sunday was, at any rate, a day to look forward to in that it was different from the other six days of the week, and although it might not on its arrival show quite so pleasant a face as earlier hours had given it, nevertheless it was something —a landmark if nothing else.

And now on this dark and dreary Monday—with the first hour a tedious and bickering discussion on Divinity, and the second hour a universal and embittered Latin exercise—that early rising to the cold summoning of the bell was anything but pleasant.

Moreover, on this especial Monday the rain came thundering in furious torrents, and the row of trees opposite the Lower School wailed and cried with their dripping, naked boughs, and all the brown leaves on the paths were beaten and flattened into a miserable and hopeless pulp.

Monday was the only morning in the week on which Traill took early preparation at the Upper School, and he had noticed before that it nearly always rained on Mondays. He was in no very bright temper as he hurried down the cold stone passages, pulling on his gown and avoiding the bodies of numerous small boys who flung themselves against him as they rushed furiously downstairs in order to be in time for call-over.

He heard the rain beating against the window-panes and hurriedly selected the first umbrella that he saw in the stand and rushed to the Upper School.

That preparation hour was unpleasant. M. Pons, the French master, was in the room above him, and the ceiling shook with the delighted stamp of twenty boys blessed with a sense of humour and an opportunity of power. M. Pons could be figured with shaking hands in the middle of the room appealing for quiet. And, as was ever the case, the spirit of rebellion passed down through the ceiling to the room beneath. Traill had his boys well under control; but whereas on ordinary occasions it was all done without effort and worked of its own accord, on this morning continual persistence was necessary, and he had to make examples of various offenders.

A preparation hour always invited the Seven Devils to dance across the two hundred of open books, and the tweaking of boys' bodies and the digging of pins into unsuspecting legs was the inevitable result. Traill rose at the end of the hour, cross, irritable, and already tired. He hurried down to the Lower School to breakfast and forgot the umbrella.

The rain was driving furiously against the window-panes of the Junior common room. The windows were tightly closed, and still the presence of yesterday's mutton was felt heavily, gloomily, about the ceiling. The brown and black oilcloth contained numberless little winds and draughts that leapt out from under it and crept here and there about the room.

A small fire was burning in the grate—a mountain of black coal and stray spirals of grey smoke, and little white edges of unburnt paper hanging from the black bars. Beyond the side door voices quarrelling in the kitchen could be heard, and beyond the other door a hum of voices and a clatter of cups.

It was all so dingy that it struck even the heavy brain of Clinton, who was down first. Perrin was taking breakfast in the big dining-room, and Traill was not yet back from the Upper School.

Clinton seized the *Daily Mirror* and, with a grunt of dissatisfaction at the general appearance of things, sat down. He never thought very intently about anything, but, in a vague way, he did dislike Monday and rain and a smoking fire. He helped himself to more than his share of the breakfast, ate it in large, noisy mouthfuls, found the *Mirror* dull, and relapsed on to the *Daily Mail*. The rain and the quarrelling in the kitchen were very disturbing.

Then Traill came in and sat down with an air of relief. He had no very great opinion of Clinton, but they got on together quite agreeably, and he found that it was rather pleasanter to have an entirely negative person with one—it was not necessary to think about him.

'My word,' said Clinton, his eyes glued to the *Daily Mail*, 'the London Scottish fairly wiped the floor with the Harlequins on Saturday—two goals and a try to a try—all that man Binton—extraordinary three-quarter—no flies on him! Have some sausages? Not bad. I wonder if they 'll catch that chap Deakin?'

'Deakin?' said Traill rather drearily, looking up from his breakfast. How dismal it all was this morning! Oh, well—in a year's time!

'Yes, you know—the Hollins Road murder—the man who cut his wife and mother into little bits and mixed them up so that they couldn't tell which was which. There 's a photograph of him here and his front door.'

'I think,' said Traill, shortly, 'following up murder trials like that is perfectly beastly. It isn't civilized.'

'All right!' said Clinton, helping himself to the remaining sausages. 'Perrin 's having breakfast in there, isn't he? He won't want any more.'

'He sometimes does,' said Traill, feeling that at the moment he hated Clinton's good-natured face more than anything in the whole world. 'He 's awfully sick if he comes in hungry and doesn't find anything.'

Clinton smiled. 'He 's rather amusing when he 's sick,' he said. 'He so often is. By the way, has the Head passed those exam. questions of yours yet?'

'No,' said Traill, frowning. 'He 's made me do them five times now, and last time he crossed out a whole lot of questions that he himself had suggested the time before. I pointed that out to him, and he called me, politely and gently, but firmly, a liar. There 's no question that he 's got his knife into me now, and I 've got friend Perrin to thank for it!'

'Yes,' said Clinton, helping himself to marmalade, 'Perrin doesn't love you—there 's no question of that. Young Garden Minimus has been helping the feud.'

'Garden? What 's he got to do with it?

'Well, you know that he was always Old

Pompous's especial pet—well, Pompous has riled him, kept him in or something, so now he goes about telling everybody that he's transferred his allegiance to you. That makes Pompous sick as anything.'

'I like the kid especially,' Traill said. 'He's rather a favourite of mine.'

'Yes,' said Clinton. 'Well, look out for trouble, that's all. There'll be open war between you soon if you are not careful.'

At that moment Perrin came in. He was continuing, as he entered, a conversation with some small boy whose head just appeared at the door for a moment and revealed Garden Minimus.

'Well, a hundred times,' Perrin was saying, 'and you don't go out till you've done it.'

Garden displayed annoyance, and was heard to mutter under his breath. Perrin's face was grey; his hair appeared to be unbrushed, and there was a good deal of white chalk on the back of his sleeve.

'Really, it's too bad,' he said to no one in particular and certainly not to Traill. 'I don't know what's come over that boy—nothing but continuous impertinence. He shall go up to the Head, if he isn't careful. Such a nice boy, too, before this term.'

At this moment he saw that Traill was reading the *Mirror* and Clinton the *Daily Mail.* He looked as though he were going to say something, then by a tremendous effort controlled himself.

He stood in front of the dismal fire and glared at the other two, at the dreary window-panes and the driving rain, at the dusty pigeon-holes, the untidy heap of books, the torn lists hanging from the walls.

He had slept badly—had lain awake for hours thinking of Miss Desart, of his own miserable condition, of his poor mother—and then, slumbering at last, in an instant he had been pulled, dragged wide-awake by that thundering, clamouring bell.

He had been so tired that his eyes had refused to open, and he had sat stupidly on the edge of his bed with his head swaying and nodding. Then he had been late for preparation, and he knew that they had been 'playing about' and had rubbed Pomfret-Walpole's head in the ink and had stamped on his body, because, although it was so early, Pomfret-Walpole's eyes were already red, his back a horrible confusion of dust and chalk, his hair and collar ink and disaster.

He was sorry for Pomfret-Walpole, whose days were a perpetual tragedy; but as there was no other obvious victim, he selected him for the subject of his wrath, expatiated to the form on the necessity of getting up clean in the morning, and sent the large, blubbering creature up to the matron to be cleansed and scolded. Verily the delights of some people's school-days have been vastly exaggerated!

Then Garden Minimus had been discovered

sticking nibs into the fleshy portion of his neighbour, and, although he had vehemently denied the crime, had been heavily punished and had therefore sulked during the rest of the hour. At breakfast-time Perrin had called him up to him and had hinted that if he chose to be agreeable once again the punishment might be relaxed; but Garden did not please, and sulked and muttered under his breath, and Perrin thought he had caught the word 'Pompous.'

All these things may have been slight in themselves, but combined they amounted to a great deal—and all before half-past eight in the morning. Also he had had very little to eat.

He had been brought a small red tomato and a hard, rocky wedge of bacon with little white eyes in it, and an iron determination to hold out at all costs, whatever the consumer's appetite and determination. He smelt, when he came into the common room, sausages, and he saw, with a glance of the eye, that there were sausages no longer.

'I really think, Clinton,' he said, 'that a little less appetite on your part in the early morning would be better for every one concerned.'

Clinton was always perfectly good-tempered, and all he said now was, 'All right, old chap—I always have an awful appetite in the morning. I always had.'

Perrin drew himself to his full height and prepared to be dignified.

Clinton said, 'I say, old man, you 've got chalk all over your sleeve.'

And Perrin, finding that it was indeed true, could say nothing and feebly tried to brush it off with his hand.

Traill had not spoken since Perrin had come in. He disliked intensely the atmosphere of restraint in the room. He had never before been on such bad terms with any one, and now at every move there were discomforts, difficulties, stiffnesses. At this moment he loathed the term and the place and the people as he had never loathed any of them before; he felt that he could not possibly last until the holidays.

Perrin was going to the Upper School for first hour. He was going to teach Divinity, the lesson that he hated most of all. He gathered his books up and his gown, and went out into the hall to find his umbrella. The rain was falling more heavily than before, and lashed the panes as though it had some personal grievance against them.

Robert, the general factotum—a long, pale man with a spotty face and a wonderful capacity for dropping china—came in to collect the breakfast things. He passed, clattering about the table. Traill was still deep in the *Mirror*.

Perrin came in with a clouded brow. 'I can't find,' he said, 'my umbrella.'

The rain beat upon the frames, Robert clashed the plates together, but there was no answer.

Clinton's head was in his pigeon-hole, looking for papers.

'Robert, have you seen my umbrella?'

No, Robert had not seen any umbrella. He might have seen an umbrella last week, somewhere upstairs, in Miss Madder's room—an umbrella with lace, pink—Oh! of course, a parasol. There were three umbrellas in the stand by the hall door. Perhaps one of those was the one. No? Mr. Perrin had looked? Well, he didn't know of anywhere else. No—perhaps one of the young gentlemen . . . There was nothing at all to be got out of Robert.

'Clinton!' No answer. 'Clinton!'

At last Clinton turned round.

'Clinton, have you seen my umbrella?'

'No, old man—why should I? Isn't it outside?'

It was getting late, the rain was pelting down, and Perrin was quite determined that he would *not* under any circumstances use any one else's umbrella.

He went out again and looked in the hall. He was beginning to get very angry. Was not this the last straw sent by the little gods to break his humble back? That it should be raining, that he should be late, and that there should be no umbrella! He stormed about the hall, he looked in impossible places, he shook the three umbrellas that were there; he began to mutter to himself—the little red and yellow china man was creeping down the stairs. He was shaking all over, and his hands were trembling like leaves.

He came into the common room again. 'I can't think——' he said, with his trembling hand to his forehead. 'I know I had it yesterday—last night. Clinton, you *must* have seen it.'

'No,' said Clinton in that abstract voice that is so profoundly irritating because it shows that the speaker's thoughts are far away. 'No—I don't think I 've seen it. What did I do with that Algebra? Oh, there it is. My word! isn't it raining!'

The Upper School bell began, far in the distance, its raucous clanging. Perrin was pacing up and down the room; every now and again he flung a furtive glance at Traill. Traill had paid, hitherto, no attention to the conversation. At last, hearing the Upper School bell, he looked up.

'What 's the matter?' he said.

'Really, Robert,' said Perrin, turning round to the factotum, 'you *must* have seen it somewhere. It 's absurd! I want to go out.'

'There are the other gentlemen's,' said Robert, looking a little frightened of Perrin's twitching lips and white face.

It dawned upon Traill slowly that Perrin was looking for an umbrella. Then on that it followed that possibly the umbrella that he had taken that morning might be Perrin's umbrella. Of course, it *must* be Perrin's umbrella. It was just the sort of umbrella, with its faded silk and stupid handle, that Perrin would be likely to have. However, it was really very awkward—most awkward.

He stood up and stayed with a hand nervously fingering the *Mirror*.

Perrin rushed once more into the hall and then came furiously back. 'I *must* have my umbrella,' he said, storming at Robert. 'I want to go to the Upper School.'

He had left the door a little open.

'I am very sorry,' Traill began; the paper crackling beneath his fingers.

Perrin wheeled round and stared at him, his face very white.

'I 'm very sorry,' said Traill again, 'but I 'm afraid I must have taken it—my mistake. I wouldn't have taken it if I had dreamed——'

'You!' said Perrin in a hoarse whisper.

'Yes,' said Traill, 'I 'm afraid I took the first one I saw this morning. I 'm afraid it must have been yours, as yours is missing. I assure you——'

He was smiling a little—really it was all too absurd. His smile drove Perrin into a trembling passion. He took a step forward.

'You dared to take my umbrella?' he said; 'without asking? I never heard such a piece of impertinence. But it 's all of a piece—all of a piece!'

'But it 's really too absurd,' Traill broke in. 'As though a man mightn't take another man's umbrella without all this disturbance! It 's too absurd.'

'Oh, is it?' said Perrin, his voice shaking. 'That 's all of a piece—that 's exactly like the rest of your behaviour here. You come here thinking that everything and every one belongs to you. Oh yes! we 've all got to bow down to everything that your Highness chooses to say. We must give up everything to your Highness—our clothes, our possessions — you conceited — insufferable puppy!'

These words were gasped out. Perrin was now entirely beside himself with rage. He saw this man here before him as the originator of all his misfortunes, all his evils. He had put the other masters against him, he had put the boys against him, he had taken Garden away from him, he had been against him at every turn.

All control, all discipline, everything had fled from Mr. Perrin. He did not remember where he was, he did not remember that Robert was in the room, he did not remember that the door was open and that the boys could hear his shrill, excited voice. He only knew that here, in this smiling, supercilious, conceited young man, was his enemy, the man who would rob and ruin him.

'Really, this is too absurd,' said Traill, stepping back a little, and conscious of the startled surprise on the face of Robert—he did not want to have a scene before a servant. 'I am exceedingly sorry that I took your umbrella. I don't see that that gives you any reason to speak to me like that. We can discuss the matter afterwards—not here.'

'Oh yes!' screamed Perrin, moving still nearer his enemy. 'Oh! of course to you it is nothing —nothing at all—it is all of a piece with the rest of your behaviour. If you don't know how to behave like a gentleman, it 's time someone taught you. Gentlemen don't steal other people's things. You can be put in prison for that sort of thing, you know.'

'I didn't steal your beastly umbrella,' said Traill, beginning in his anger to forget the ludicrousness of the situation. 'I don't want your beastly things—keep them to yourself.'

'I say'—this from Clinton—'chuck it, you two. Don't make such a row here—every one can hear. Wait until later.'

But Perrin heard nothing. He had stepped up to Traill now and was shaking his fist in Traill's face.

'It 's beastly, is it?' he shouted. 'I 'll give you something for saying that—I 'll let you know.' And then, in a perfect scream, 'Give me my umbrella! Give me my umbrella!'

'I haven't got your rotten umbrella,' shouted Traill. 'I left it somewhere. I 've lost it. I 'm jolly glad. You can jolly well go and look for it.'

And at this moment, as Clinton afterwards described it, 'the scrap began.' Perrin suddenly flung himself upon Traill and beat his face with his fist. Traill clutched Perrin's arm and flung him back upon the breakfast - table. Perrin's head struck the coffee-pot, and as he rose he brought with him the table-cloth and all the things that Robert had left upon the table. With a fearful crash of crockery, with the odour of streaming coffee, with the cry of the terrified Robert, down everything came. Afterwards there was a pause whilst Perrin and Traill swayed together, then with another crash they too came to the floor.

Clinton and Robert rushed forward. Two Upper School masters, Birkland and Comber, surveyed the scene from the doorway. There was an instant's absolute silence.

Then suddenly Traill and Perrin both rose from the floor. Traill's lip was cut and bleeding —coffee was on Perrin's collar; their faces were very white.

For a moment they looked at each other in absolute silence, then they passed, without a spoken word, through the open door.

In such a way, and from such a cause, did this Battle of the Umbrella have its beginning.

CHAPTER VIII

THE BATTLE OF THE UMBRELLA: CAMPS ARE FORMED—ALSO SOME SKIRMISHING

I

ISABEL DESART heard about it early on the afternoon of the same day. Traill himself told her as he stood with her for a moment outside the school gates before he went down to football.

She saw it at once more seriously than he did; his attitude had been that it was a pity, above all that it was indecorous, that he had, in a way, made a fool of himself—that to struggle in that fashion with a man like Perrin before an audience was a pity. But to her it was a great deal more than this. In many ways she was older than Archie Traill, and her feminine intuition helped her now; she saw Perrin as something to be feared and also something to be pitied, and she did not know which of these feelings was the stronger. She had always seen Perrin as someone to be pitied—that was the reason of her kindness to him—and now that he was ludicrous, now that this climax had made him prominent, her pity for him was increased.

But she was also afraid. She guessed suddenly a great deal more than she could actually see; she felt the miserable years that he had been through, she felt his hatred of his own position, and she knew that he would not be likely to forgive the man who had brought all this to a climax.

They were all at such terribly close quarters. It would be easy enough to get away from that sort of incident if they all of them were, as she put it to herself, 'spread out'; but half-term was only just over, and she did not know what the next six weeks might bring. Traill's feeling, she saw, was mainly one of disgust—the same kind of sensation that he would have had if he had not been able to have his bath in the morning. About Perrin he only felt contempt; a man who could make that kind of disturbance about so small a thing . . .

Traill's final opinion, in fact, about it all was that 'it wasn't done' and that Perrin was therefore an 'outsider,' and that there the thing ended.

Isabel, in the few words that he had time to say to her, saw all this and knew that his attitude would not make the whole affair any easier. But she was wise enough to leave it all where it was for the moment and simply to tell him that she was sorry.

'One thing, you know,' she said, smiling at him and blushing a little. 'We must let them all know about us, at once, to-day.'

'Oh! must we?' he said, shrinking back a little.

'Why, of course. You don't suppose there isn't going to be talk about all this business. Of course there is, heaps—and you must let me do my share of standing up for you. I must have the right, you know.'

He had not figured the talk that there would be—he saw it all now in an instant, that there would be sides and discussions, and, looking further still, he had some idea of all the issues that were to be involved; but he was much too simple a person to think this further vision anything but fantastic: people simply didn't fight to that extent about umbrellas. . . .

He left her with a smiling consent to the announcement of their engagement, and, for the moment, the thought of that swallowed all the Perrin affair. He went down to his football cheerfully.

II

Meanwhile, in the Senior common room, during that interval between Chapel and dinner, things had occurred. The news of the morning struggle had been brought, of course, by the eager witnesses, Comber and Birkland, much earlier in the day; but the school day was a very busy one—one hour followed another with terrible swiftness, and then there were boys to see and games to play and all the accumulated details to fill in any odd moments that there might be—so that with the exception of short sentences and exclamations and a general air of pleasurable surprise pervading everything, no real movement was possible until this evening hour. The room, lighted by gas, was more ugly and naked than ever; although it was close and stuffy, the spirit of it was cold and chill.

Comber was in the chair of honour, the only arm-chair in the room; Birkland and Pons, White and Dormer, and the little science master, West, were also there. Little West was so obvious and striking an example of his type that it seemed as though he had been specially created to stand to the end of time as an example of what a Board School education and a pushing disposition can do for a man. He was short and square, with a shaggy, unkempt moustache and that sallow, unhealthy complexion that two generations of ill-fed progenitors tend to produce. He was a little bald on the top of his head, wore ready-made clothes, and spoke slowly and with great care. He had worked exceedingly hard all his youth and was the only master at Moffatt's whose ambitions were unimpaired and optimism (concerning his own future) unchecked. His most striking feature was his hard, burning little eyes, and it was with these that he kept order in class.

He disliked all the other members of the staff, but he hated Birkland. Birkland had, from the first, laughed at him; he had laughed at his clothes, at his accent, at his pretensions to being a gentleman (to do Birkland justice, if West had never pretended to be a gentleman at all, he would have admired and liked him). In fact, he made him his chief and principal butt; and West, being slow of speech and (outside his own subject) slow of brain, could never reply anything at all to Birkland's sallies, and was left helpless and fuming.

Comber was reciting for the hundredth time what it was that he had seen. The whole affair gave him very particular pleasure; he thought Traill a conceited, insufferable young man, who had come in and taken the football out of his hands and supplanted him completely—whenever he thought of it he boiled over with rage; but he had never been able to do anything, because Traill had never given himself away. He played football a great deal better than Comber even in his palmiest days had ever played it. Traill had given him no opportunity until now; but now at last Comber glowed with the thought of the things that he would be able to do. He intended it in no way maliciously—it was simply that the younger generation should be taught its place; let Traill once submit to Comber's rule in the football world and Comber would be pleasant enough. Then Comber did not like Birkland's sharp tongue any more than the rest of the staff did, and Birkland was a friend of Traill's. Of course, on the other side, Comber did not like Perrin either. Perrin was a pompous, pretentious fool, but in this case it was clearly Comber's duty to uphold the senior staff.

He was leaning back in his arm-chair, with his chest out and one finger impressively in the air. 'There they were, you know, rolling—positively rolling—on the floor. And all the breakfast things broken to bits and the coffee streaming all over the floor—you never saw anything like it. And then up they both got and looked at each other, and went out of the room without a word, brushing past Birkland and me as though we weren't there; didn't they, Birkland?'

Birkland was sitting in his chair with a sad, rather cynical smile on his face, as though he were saying, 'This is their kind of life. Look at Comber there, now—how pleased he is with things! Will be happy for a month at least, and all their little private hates and jealousies are being fed just as you feed the snakes at the Zoo. And aren't I just as bad as the rest? Aren't I pleased, because it will give me a chance of having a hit at the rest of them? . . . What a set we are!'

But he didn't say anything—he just sat there listening, with his contemptuous smile, to Comber.

'An awful noise, you know, they made,' Comber went on. 'And anything funnier than Perrin when he got up you never saw, with his hair all tousled and pulled about, and dust all over his back, and his cheek bleeding where the coffee-pot had hit him. My word, it was funny!'

'At all events,' said Birkland dryly, 'we ought

all to be glad that you got such amusement out of it, Comber. That 's something to be thankful for, at any rate.'

'Oh, it 's all very well, Birkland,' Comber answered angrily; 'you were amused enough yourself, really—you know you were. In any case,' he went on importantly, 'the thing can't go on, you know. We can't have junior masters flinging themselves at the throats of senior ones. That sort of thing must be stopped.'

So it was at once apparent on whose side Comber was, and every one trimmed his sails accordingly. If one disliked Comber sufficiently and was not afraid of him, one would, of course, for the moment, side with Traill; and supposing one wished to get into Comber's good graces (no easy thing to do), here would be an excellent opportunity. M. Pons, for instance, thought so.

'It is—*dégoûtant*,' he cried, waving his hands in the air, 'that a young man, that is here one month, two months, should catch the throat of his senior. These things,' he added with the air of one who waves gloriously the flag of the Republic, 'are not done in my country.'

'Well, when they are, perhaps you 'll be able to judge of them better, Pons,' said Birkland. 'Until then, I should recommend silence.'

M. Pons flushed angrily, but made no reply, and then looked appealingly at Comber.

'Of course, Birkland,' said Comber, 'if you are going to encourage that sort of spirit in the staff, one has nothing to say. I dare say you would like all the boys to be springing at one another's throats in the same way; if that 's what you want, well——'; and he waved his hands expressively.

'It 's absurd,' said Birkland quietly, 'of Perrin to have made such a fuss. As if a man mayn't borrow another man's umbrella without being struck in the face. It 's more than absurd, it 's childish. It 's just the sort of thing that Perrin *would* do.'

'Very well,' said Comber; 'let Perrin treat you in the way that Traill 's treated him, and you see what you 'd say and do. All I know is that you wouldn't stand it for a minute, you of all men, Birkland.'

'What do you mean by that?' Birkland said hotly.

'Oh, well, we all know you haven't got the sweetest of tempers, old man,' Comber said, laughing. 'You can't lay claim to good temper whatever else you may have.'

West laughed also and seemed to enjoy the joke immensely.

'Of course, you 're on the side of authority, West,' Birkland said. 'You naturally would be.' West was all the more annoyed because he didn't in the least understand what Birkland meant.

The atmosphere began to be warm. But Comber despised West as an ally and did not think very much of M. Pons, so he turned round to White. White was sitting, as he always did, quietly in the background, without saying anything. He was so quiet that people often forgot that he was there at all. The effect of many years' bullying by Moy-Thompson was to make him agree eagerly with the opinion of the last speaker, and therefore Comber hadn't any doubt about the support that he would receive. But White had never forgotten that hand-clasp that Traill had given him, and now, to every one's intense surprise, he said, 'I think Birkland 's perfectly right. A man oughtn't to lose his temper because another man 's borrowed his umbrella. I think Traill 's been very hardly used—at any rate, we all know what Perrin must be to live with.'

Every one was surprised, and Comber so astonished that for some time he could find no words at all.

At last he broke out, 'Well, all I can say is that you people don't know what you are in for; if you go on encouraging people like Traill to go about stealing people's things——'

'Look here, Comber,' Birkland broke in. 'You 've no right to say stealing. You may as well try and be fair. Traill never stole anything; you 'd better be more careful of your words.'

'Well, I call it stealing, anyhow,' said Comber hotly. 'You can call it what you like, Birkland. I dare say you 've got pet words of your own for these things. But when a man takes something that isn't his and keeps it——'

'He didn't keep it,' Birkland said angrily.

'You 're grossly prejudiced, just as you always are.'

'What about yourself?' West broke in. 'People in glass houses——'

At this point the temperature of the room became very warm indeed. Comber was pale with rage; he had never been so grossly insulted before—not that it very much mattered what a wretched creature like Birkland said.

He began to explain in a loud voice that some people weren't fit to be in gentlemen's society, and that though, of course, he wouldn't like to mention names, nevertheless, if certain persons thought about it long enough, they would probably find that the cap fitted, and that if only people could occasionally see themselves as others saw them—well, it might be better for every one concerned, and then perhaps there would be a chance of their behaving decently in decent society, although of course, if one's education had been neglected . . .

Meanwhile, M. Pons was explaining to West that whether you went in for science or modern languages one's opinion of this sort of affair must be the same, there was no question about it.

Birkland was sitting back, white and stiff, in his chair and wishing that he might take all their heads and crash them together in one big debacle.

Then suddenly, when another two minutes might have been dangerous for every one concerned, the door was flung open and Clinton entered. He was excited, he was stirred; it was obvious that he had news.

'I say!' he cried, and then stopped All eyes were upon him.

'What do you think?' he cried again. 'Traill has just told me. He's engaged to Miss Desart.'

At that there was dead silence—for an instant nobody spoke. Then Comber got up from his chair. 'Well, I'm damned!' he said.

This was a new development; it is hard to say whether he saw at once then the domestic complications into which it would lead him. Miss Desart had stayed with them again and again; she was their intimate friend. His wife was devoted to her and would, of course, at once espouse her cause. But this piece of news made him, Comber, even angrier than he had been before. His feeling about the engagement defied analysis, but it rested in some curious, hidden way on some strange streak of vanity in him. He had always cared very especially for Miss Desart; he had given her, in his clumsy, heavy way, little attentions and regards that he gave to very few people. He had always thought that she had very great admiration and reverence for himself, and now she had engaged herself, without a word to him about it, to someone whom he disliked and disapproved of. He was hurt and displeased, he knew that his wife would be delighted—more trouble at home. Here was White openly insulting him in the common room;

he was called names by Birkland; a nice, pleasant girl had defied him (it had already come to that); his wife would probably defy him also in an hour or two. With a muttered word or two, he left the gathering.

For the others, this engagement was a piquant development that lent a new colour to everything. They had all noticed that Mr. Perrin cared for Miss Desart, and now this sudden dramatic announcement was another knock in the face for that poor, battered gentleman. Of course, she would never have accepted him; but, nevertheless, it was rather hard that she should be handed over to his hated rival.

'Does Perrin know?' was West's eager question.

'No,' said Clinton, smiling, 'I 'm just going to tell him.'

III

Meanwhile, there is our Mr. Perrin sitting very drearily and alone in front of his sombre fire. As he sat there it wasn't that he was so much depressed by the morning's affair as that he was so frightened by it—not frightened because of anything that Traill could do, or indeed of anything that any one could very especially say: he was long past the terror of tongues—but rather afraid of himself and the way that he might be going to behave.

He had long ago, when he was a very young

man indeed, recognized that there were two Mr. Perrins; indeed, in all probability, more than two. He knew that when he had been quite a boy he had had ideas of being a hero—a hero, of course, just as other young things meant to be heroes, with a great deal of recognition and trumpets and bands and one's face in the papers. He had, moreover, in those days, a stern and ready belief in his own powers and judged, from a comparison of himself with other boys, that he was really promising and had a future. He had heard some preacher in a sermon—he went to sermons very often in those days—say that every man had, once at any rate during his lifetime, his chance, and that it was his own fault if he missed it; that very often people did not know that it had ever come, because they had not been looking out for it, and then they cursed Fate when it was really their own fault—all this Perrin remembered, and he would lie awake at nights on the watch for this chance — this splendid moment.

That was one Mr. Perrin; rather a fine one, with a great desire to do the right thing, with a very great love for his mother, and with rather a pathetic anxiety to have friends and affection and to do good.

Then there was the other Mr. Perrin—the ill-tempered, pompous, sarcastic, bitter Mr. Perrin. When Perrin No. 1 was uppermost, he recognized and deeply regretted Perrin No. 2; but when

Perrin No. 2 was in command he saw nothing but a spiteful and malignant world trying, as he phrased it, to 'do him down.'

Now, as he sat sadly by his fire, he saw them both. That Mr. Perrin this morning had, of course, been Perrin No. 2, and Perrin No. 2 very fierce and strong and warlike. Perrin No. 1 was afraid. If this sort of thing continued, then Perrin No. 1 would disappear altogether. This term had been worse than ever, and he had begun it with so strong a determination to make a good thing of it! This young Traill—and then Perrin No. 2 showed his head again, and the room grew dark and there was thunder in the air. But, oh, if he could only have his chance! If he could only prove the kind of man that he *could* be! If he could only get out of this, away from it—if someone would take him away from it: he did not feel strong enough, after all these years, to go away by himself. And then, suddenly, he thought of Miss Desart. He saw her as his shining light, his beacon. There was his salvation; he would make her love him and care for him. He would show her the kind of man that he could be; and then at the thought of it he began to smile, and a little colour crept into his pale cheeks, and he felt that if only that were possible, he might be quite pleasant to Traill and the rest. Oh, they would matter so little!

He nodded humorously to the little man on the mantelpiece and fell into a delicious reverie.

He forgot the quarrel of the morning, the insults that he had received, all the talk that there would be, all the opportunities that it would give to his enemies to say what they thought about him. And then, perhaps, with her by his side, he might rise to great things; he would have a little house, there would be children, he would be his own master, life would be free, splendid, tranquil. He could make her so fond of him—he was sure that he could; there were sides of him that no one had ever seen, even his mother did not know all that was in him.

Perrin No. 1 filled the dingy room with his radiance. There was a knock on the door. Clinton came in, a pipe in his mouth, a book in his hand.

'Oh, here 's your Algebra that you lent me. I meant to have returned it before.'

'Oh, thanks!' Perrin was always rather short with Clinton. 'Won't you sit down?'

'No, thanks, I'm taking prep.' Nevertheless, Clinton lingered a little, talking about nothing in particular; he stood by the mantelpiece, fingering things, a practice that always annoyed Perrin intensely—then he took up the little china man and looked at him. 'Rum chap that,' he said. 'Well, chin-chin——' He moved off; he stood for a moment by the door. 'Oh, I say!' he said, half turning round, his hand on the handle; 'have you heard the news? Traill 's engaged to Miss Desart. He 's just told me.' He looked at Perrin for a moment, and then went out, banging the door behind him.

Perrin did not move; his hands began to shake; then suddenly his head fell between his shoulders, and his body heaved with sobs. He sat there for a long time, then he began to pace his room; his steps were faster and faster—he was like a wild animal in a cage.

Suddenly he stopped in front of the little china man. His face was white, his eyes were large and staring; with a wild gesture he picked the thing up and flung it to the ground, where it lay at his feet, smashed into atoms. . . .

CHAPTER IX

THE BATTLE OF THE UMBRELLA: WITH THE LADIES

I

ISABEL told Mrs. Comber on that same afternoon at tea-time; but that good lady, owing to the interruption of the other good ladies and her own Mr. Comber, was unable to say anything really about it until just before going to bed. Mrs. Comber would not have been able to say very much about it in any case quite at first, because her breath was so entirely taken away by surprise, and then afterwards by delight and excitement. For herself this term had, so far, been rather a difficult affair: money had been hard, and Freddie had been even harder—and hard, as she complained, in such strange, tricky corners—never when you would expect him to be and always when you wouldn't. This Mrs. Comber considered terribly unfair, because if one knew what he was going to mind, one would look out for it and be especially careful; but when he let irritating things pass without a word and then 'flew out' when there was nothing for any one to be distressed about, life became a hideous series of nightmares with the enemy behind every hedge.

Mrs. Comber knew that this term had been worse than usual, because she had arrived already, although it was only just past half-term, at the condition of saying nothing to Freddie when he spoke to her—she called it submission, but she never arrived at it until she was nearly at the limits of her endurance. And now this news of Isabel suddenly made the world bright again; she loved Isabel better than any one in the world except Freddie and the children; and her love was of the purely unselfish kind, so that joy at Isabel's happiness far outweighed her own discomforts. She was really most tremendously glad, glad with all her size and volubility and colour.

Isabel talked to her in her bedroom—it was of course also Freddie's, but he had left no impression on it whatever, whereas *she*, by a series of touches—the light green wall-paper and the hard black of the shining looking-glass, the silver things, and the china things (not very many, but all made the most of)—had made it her own unmistakably, so that everything shouted Mrs. Comber with a war of welcome. It was indeed, in spite of the light green paper, a noisy impression, and one had always the feeling that things—the china, the silver, and the chairs—jumped when one wasn't in, charged, as it were, with the electricity of Mrs. Comber's temperament and the colour of her dresses.

But of course Isabel knew it all well enough, and she didn't in the least mind the stridency of it—in fact it all rather suited the sense of battle that there was in the air, so that the things seemed to say that they knew that there was a row on, and that they jolly well liked it. Freddie had been cross at dinner, and so, in so far as it was at all his room, the impression would not have been pleasant; but he just, one felt, slipped into bed and out of it, and there was an end of his being there.

Mrs. Comber, taking a few things off, putting a bright new dressing-gown on, and smiling from ear to ear, watched Isabel with burning eyes.

'Oh, my dear! . . . No, just come and sit on the bed beside me and have these things off, and I've been much too busy to write about that skirt of mine that I told you I would, and there it is hanging up to shame me! Well! I'm just too glad, you dear!' Here she hugged and kissed and patted her hand. 'And he is *such* a nice young man, although Freddie doesn't like him, you know, over the football or something, although I'm sure I never know what men's reasons are for disliking one another, and Freddie's especially; but I liked him ever since he dined here that night, although I didn't really see much of him because, you know, he played Bridge at the other table and I was *much* too worried!' She drew a breath, and then added quite simply, like a child, and in that way of hers that was so perfectly fascinating: 'My dear, I love you, and I want you to be happy, and I think you will—and I want *you* to love *me.*'

Isabel could only, for answer, fling her arms about her and hold her very tight indeed, and she felt in that little confession that there was more pathos than any one human being could realize and that life was very hard for some people.

'Of course, it is wonderful,' she said at last, looking with her clear, beautiful eyes straight in front of her. 'One never knew how wonderful until it actually came. Love is more than the finest writer has ever said and not, I suspect, quite so much as the humblest lover has ever thought—and that 's pessimistic of me, I suppose,' she added, laughing; 'but it only means that I 'm up to all the surprises and ready for them.'

'You 'll find it exactly whatever you make it,' Mrs. Comber said slowly. 'I don't think the other party has really very much to do with it. You never lose what you give, my dear; but, as a matter of fact, he 's the very nicest and trustiest young man, and no one could ever be a brute to you, whatever kind of brutes they were to any one else—and I wish I 'd remembered about that skirt.'

The silence of the room and house, the peace of the night outside, came about Isabel like a comfortable cloak, so that she believed that everything was most splendidly right.

'And now, my dear,' said Mrs. Comber, 'tell

me what this is that I hear about your young man and Mr. Perrin, because I only heard the veriest words from Freddie, and I was just talking to Jane at the time about not breathing when she 's handing round the things, because she 's always doing it, and she 'll have to go if she doesn't learn.'

Isabel looked grave.

'It seems the silliest affair,' she said; 'and yet it 's a great pity, because it may make a lot of trouble, I 'm afraid. But that 's why we announced our engagement to-day, because it 'll be, it appears, a case of taking sides.'

'It always is here,' said Mrs. Comber, 'when there 's the slightest opportunity of it.'

'Well, it looks as though there were going to be plenty of opportunity this time,' Isabel said, sighing. 'It really is *too* silly. Apparently Archie took Mr. Perrin's umbrella to preparation in Upper School this morning without asking. They hadn't been getting on very well before, and when Mr. Perrin asked for his umbrella and Archie said that he'd taken it, there was a regular fight. The worst of it is that there were lots of people there; and now, of course, it is all over the school, and it will never be left alone as it ought to be.'

'My dear,' said Mrs. Comber solemnly, 'it will be the opportunity for all sorts of things. We're all just ripe for it. How perfectly absurd of Mr. Perrin! But then he 's an ass, and I always said so, and now it only proves it, and I wish he'd never come here. Of course you know that I'm with you, my dear; but I'm afraid that Freddie won't be, because he doesn't like your Archie, and there's no getting over it—and on whose side all the others will be there's no knowing whatever—and indeed I don't like to think of it all.'

She was so serious about it that Isabel at once became serious too. Her worst suspicions about it were suddenly confirmed, so that the room, instead of its quiet and peace, was filled with a thousand sharp terrors and crawling fears. She was afraid of Mr. Perrin, she was afraid of the crowd of people, she was afraid of all the ill-feeling that promised soon to overwhelm her. She clutched Mrs. Comber's arm.

'Oh!' she cried, 'will they hate us?'

'They 'll do their best, my dear,' said that lady solemnly, 'to hate somebody.'

II

And they came, comparatively in their multitudes, to tea on the next afternoon.

Tuesday was, as it happened, Mrs. Comber's day, and the hour's relief that followed its ending scarcely outweighed the six days' terror at its horrible approach. Its disagreeable qualities were, of course, in the first place those of any 'at home' whatever—the stilted and sterile fact of being there sacrificially for any one to trample on in the presence of a delighted audience and a glittering tea-table. But in Mrs. Comber's case there was the additional trouble of 'town' and 'school' never in the least suiting, although 'town' was only a question of local houses like the squire and the clergyman, and they ought to have combined, one would have thought, easily enough.

The society of small provincial towns has been made again and again the jest and mockery of satiric fiction, having, it is considered, in the quality of its conversation a certain tinkling and malicious chatter that is unequalled elsewhere. Far be it from me to describe the conversation of the ladies of Moffatt's in this way—it was a thing of far deeper and graver import.

The impossibility of escape until the term's triumphant conclusion made what might, in a wider and finer hemisphere, have been simply malicious conversation that sprang up and disappeared without result, a perpetual battle of death and disaster. No slightest word but had its weightiest result, because every one was so close upon every one else that things said rebounded like peas flung against a board.

Mrs. Comber, at her tea-parties, had long ago ceased to consider the safety or danger of anything that she might say. It seemed to her that whatever she said always went wrong, and did the greatest damage that it was possible for any one thing to do; and now she counted her

Tuesdays as days of certain disaster, allowing a dozen blunders to a Tuesday and hoping that she would 'get off,' so to speak, on that. But on occasions like the present, when there was really something to talk about, she shuddered at the possible horrors; her line, of course, was strong enough, because it was Isabel first and Isabel last; and if that brought her into contact with all the other ladies of the establishment, then she couldn't help it. Had it been merely a question of the Umbrella Riot, as some wit had already phrased it, she knew clearly enough where they were all likely to be; but now that there was Isabel's engagement as well, she felt that their anger would be stirred by that bright young lady having made a step forward and having been, in some odd, obscure, feminine way, impertinently pushing.

She wished passionately, as she sat in glorious purple before her silver tea-things, her little pink cakes, and her vanishingly thin pieces of bread-and-butter, that the 'town' would, on this occasion at any rate, put in an appearance, because that would prevent any one really 'getting at' things; but, of course, as it happened, the 'town' for once wasn't there at all, and the battle raged quite splendidly.

The combatants were the two Misses Madder, Mrs. Dormer, and Mrs. Moy-Thompson, and it might seem that these ladies were not numerically enough to do any lasting serious damage; but it was the bodies that they represented rather than the individuals that they actually were; and poor Mrs. Comber, as she smiled at them and talked at them and wished that the little pink cakes might poison them all, knew exactly the reason of their separate appearances and the danger that they were, severally and individually.

The Misses Madder represented the matrons, and they represented them as securely and confidently as though they had sat in conclave already and drawn up a list of questions to be asked and answers to be given. Mrs. Dormer represented the wives and also, separately, Mrs. Dormer in so far as her own especial dislike of Mrs. Comber went for everything; Mrs. Moy-Thompson, above all, faded, black, thin, and miserable, represented her lord and master, and was regarded by the other ladies as a spy whose accurate report of the afternoon's proceedings would send threads spinning from that dark little study for the rest of the term.

The elder Miss Madder, stout, good-natured, comfortable, had not of herself any malice at all; but her thin, bony sister, exact in her chair, and with eyes looking straight down her nose, influenced her stouter sister to a wonderful extent.

The thin Miss Madder's remark on receiving her tea, 'Well, so Miss Desart 's engaged to Mr. Traill!' showed immediately which of the two pieces of news was considered the more important.

'Yes,' said Mrs. Comber, 'and I 'm sure it 's delightful. Do have one of those little pink cakes, Mrs. Thompson; they 're quite fresh; and I want you especially to notice that little water-colour over there by the screen, because I bought it in Truro last week for simply nothing at Pinner's, and I believe it 's quite a good one—I 'm sure we 're all delighted.'

Mrs. Dormer wasn't so certain. 'They 're a little young,' she said in so chilly a voice that she might have been suddenly transferred, against her will, in the dead of night in the thinnest attire, into the heart of Siberia. 'And what 's this I hear from my husband about Mr. Perrin and Mr. Traill tumbling about on the floor together this morning — something about an umbrella?'

'Yes,' said Mrs. Thompson, moving her chair a little closer, 'I heard something this morning about it.'

Mrs. Comber had never before disliked this thin, faded lady so intensely as she did on this afternoon—she seemed to chill the room with her presence; and the consciousness of the trouble that she would bring to various innocent persons in that place by the report of the things that they had said, made of her something inhuman and detached. Mrs. Comber's only way of easing the situation, 'Do have another little pink cake, Mrs. Thompson,' failed altogether on this occasion, and she could only stare at her in a fascinated kind of horror until she realized with a start that she was intended as hostess to give an account of the morning's proceedings. But she turned to Miss Madder. 'You were down there, Miss Madder; tell us all about it.'

Miss Madder was only too ready, having been in the hall at the time and having heard what she called 'the first struggle,' and having yielded eventually, rather against her better instincts, to her feminine curiosity—having in fact looked past the shoulders of Mr. Comber and Mr. Birkland and seen the gentlemen struggling on the floor.

'Actually on the floor?' said Mrs. Dormer, still in Siberia.

'Yes, actually on the floor—also all the breakfast things and coffee all over the table-cloth.'

Miss Madder was checked in her enthusiasm by her consciousness of the cold eye of Mrs. Thompson, and the possibility of being dismissed from her position at the end of the term if she said anything she oughtn't to—also the possibility of an unpleasant conversation with her clever sister afterwards. However, she considered it safe enough to offer it as her opinion that both gentlemen had forgotten themselves, and that Mr. Traill was very much younger than Mr. Perrin, although Mr. Perrin was the harder one to live with—and that it had been a clean table-cloth that morning.

'I call it disgraceful,' was the only light that

the younger Miss Madder would throw upon the question.

For a moment there was silence, and then Mrs. Dormer said, 'And really about an umbrella?'

'I understand,' said Miss Madder, who was warming to her work and beginning to forget Mrs. Thompson's eye, 'that Mr. Traill borrowed Mr. Perrin's umbrella without asking permission, and that there was a dispute.'

But it was at once obvious that what interested the ladies was the question of Miss Desart's engagement to Mr. Traill, and the effect that that had upon the disturbance in question.

'I never quite liked Mr. Traill,' said Mrs. Dormer decisively; 'and I cannot say that I altogether congratulate Miss Desart—and I must say that the quarrel of this morning looks a little as though Mr. Traill's temper was uncertain.'

'Very uncertain indeed, I should think,' said the younger Miss Madder, with a sniff.

Mrs. Comber felt their eyes upon her; she knew that they wished to know what she had to say about it all, but she was wise enough to hold her peace.

The other ladies then devoted all their energies upon getting an opinion from Mrs. Comber. During the next quarter of an hour, every lady understanding every other lady, a combined attack was made.

Semi-Chorus a.—The question of the umbrella was, of course, a question of order, and, as Mrs.

Dormer put it, when a younger master attacks an older one and flings him to the ground, and rubs his hair in the dust, and that before a large audience, the whole system of education is in danger; there 's no knowing when things will begin or end, and other masters will be doing dreadful things, and then the prefects, and then other boys, and finally a dreadful picture of the First and Second boys showing what they can do with knives and pistols.

Miss Madder entirely agreed with this, and then enlarged further on the question of property.

Semi-Chorus β.—One had one's things—here she was sure Mrs. Comber would agree—and if one didn't keep a tight hold of them in these days, one simply didn't know where one would be. Of course one umbrella was a small thing; but, after all, it *was* aggravating on a wet morning not to find it and then to have no excuse whatever offered to one—any one would be cross about it. And, after all, with some people, if you gave them an inch they took an ell, as the saying was, and if one didn't show firmness over a small thing like this, it would only lead to people taking other things without asking until one really didn't know where one was. Of course, it was a pity that Mr. Perrin should have lost his self-control as completely as he appeared to have done, but nevertheless one could quite understand how aggravating it was.

Semi-Chorus α, Mrs. Dormer, continued, keeping order was no light matter, and if those masters who had been in a school for twenty years were to be openly derided before boys and masters, if umbrellas were to be indiscriminately stolen, and if in fact anything was to be done by anybody at any time whatever without by your leave or for your leave, then one might just as well pack up one's boxes and go home; and then what would happen, one would like to know, to our schools, our boys, and finally, with an emphatic rattle of cup and saucer, to our country?

Semi-Chorus β enlarged the original issue. It was really rather difficult when a young man had been behaving in this way to congratulate the young lady to whom he had just engaged himself. She was of course perfectly charming, but it was a pity that she should, whilst still so young, be forced to countenance disorder and tumult, because with that kind of beginning there was no telling what married life mightn't develop into.

Semi-Chorus α enlarged yet again on this subject and, without mentioning names or being in any way specific, drew a dreadful picture of married lives that had been ruined simply through this question of discipline, and that if the husband were the kind of man who believed in blows and riot and general disturbance, then the wife was in for an exceedingly poor time.

Mrs. Comber had listened to this discussion in perfect silence. It was not her habit to listen to anything in perfect silence, but on the present occasion she continued to enforce in her mind that dark ominous figure of Mrs. Thompson. Anything that she said would be used against her, and there in the corner, with her thin, white hands folded in her lap, with the black silk of her dress shining in little white lines where the light caught it, was the person who might undo her Freddie entirely. Whatever happened, she must keep silence—she told herself this again and again; but as Mrs. Dormer and Miss Madder continued, she found her anger rising. She fixed her eyes on the sharp, black feathers in Miss Madder's hat and tried to discuss with herself the general expense of the hat and why Miss Madder always wore things that didn't suit her, and whether Miss Madder wouldn't be ever so much better in a nice green grave with daisies and church bells in the distance, but these abstract questions refused to allow themselves to be discussed. She knew as she listened that Isabel, her dear, beloved Isabel, to whom she owed more than any one in the whole world, was being attacked—cruelly, wickedly attacked.

Every word that came from their lips increased her rage: they hated Isabel—Isabel who had never done them any harm or hurt. As their voices, even and cold, went on, she forgot that dark silent figure in the corner, and her hands began to twitch the silk of her purple gown. Suddenly in an instant Freddie was forgotten, everything was forgotten save Isabel, and she burst out, her eyes burning, her cheeks flaming: 'Really, Mrs. Dormer, you are a little inaccurate. I 'm sure we must all agree that it 's a pity if any one is so silly as to knock someone else down because someone else has stolen one's umbrella, and I 'm sure I should never want to; and indeed I remember quite well Miss Tweedy, who was matron here two years ago, taking a grey parasol of mine to chapel with her and putting it up before everybody, and nobody thought anything of it, and I remember Miss Tweedy being quite angry because I asked for it back again. I think it 's very stupid of Mr. Perrin to make such a fuss about nothing, and I never did like him, and I don't care who knows it; but at any rate I don't see what this has all got to do with dear Isabel's engagement, and I think young Traill 's a delightful fellow, and I hope they 'll both be enormously happy, and I think it 's very unkind of you to wish them not to be!' Mrs. Comber took a deep breath.

'Really, my dear Mrs. Comber,' said Mrs. Dormer very slowly, 'I 'm sure we none of us wish them anything but happiness. Please don't have the impression that we are not eager for their good.'

'I can't help feeling, Mrs. Comber,' said Miss Madder, 'that you have rather misunderstood our position in the matter.'

'Well, I 'm sure I 'm very sorry if I have,' broke

in Mrs. Comber hurriedly, beginning already to be sorry that she had spoken so quickly.

'You see,' went on Miss Madder, 'that I don't think we can any of us have two feelings about the question of discipline. I 'm sure you agree with us there, Mrs. Comber.'

'Oh, of course,' said Mrs. Comber.

But she saw at once that war had been declared. They hated Isabel, and they hated her; they would make it so unpleasant that Isabel would not be able to come and stay again—they were of one mind.

Above all, after they had gone, there remained the impression of that silent black lady who had said not a word. What would she tell Moy-Thompson? What harm would come to Freddie?

Last, and worst of all, as Mrs. Comber most wretchedly reflected, Freddie had still to be faced.

His feelings, she knew, would be strongly expressed, and were certainly not in line with her own.

Oh, the umbrella had a great deal to answer for!

III

And Freddie was, as a matter of fact, faced that very evening, and a crisis arrived in the affairs of the Combers which must be chronicled, because it had ultimately a good deal to do with Isabel and Archie Traill, and indeed with every one in the present story.

But whilst waiting for him downstairs, 'dressed and shining,' as she used to like to say—with the dinner getting cold (for which disaster she was certain to be scolded)—she wondered in her muddled kind of way why it was that they should all have wanted to be so disagreeable, why, as a development of that, every one always preferred to be disagreeable rather than pleasant. And she suddenly, facing the ormolu clock and the peacock screen with her eyes upon them as though they might, with their colour and decoration, help her, had a revelation—dim, misty, vague, and lost almost as soon as it was seen—that it wasn't really any one's fault at all—that it was the system, the place, the tightness and closeness and helplessness that did for everybody; that nobody could escape from it, and that the finest saint, the most noble character, would be crushed and broken in that remorseless mill—'the mills of the gods?'—no, the mills of a rotten, impoverished, antiquated system. . . . She saw, staring at the clock and the screen, and clinging to them, these men and these women, crushed, beaten, defeated: Mrs. Thompson, Mrs. Dormer, Miss Madder, her own Freddie, Mr. Perrin, Mr. Birkland, Mr. White—even already young Traill—all of them decent, hopeful, brave . . . once. The coals clicked in the glowing fire, and the soft autumn wind passed down the darkening paths. She felt suddenly as though she must give it all up—she must leave Freddie and the children and go away . . . anywhere . . . she could not endure it any longer. And then Freddie came in, irritable, peevish, scarcely noticing her. Moy-Thompson had changed one of his hours, and that annoyed him; the soup of course was stone cold, the fish very little better. He scowled across the table at her, and she tried to be pleasant and amusing. Then suddenly he had launched into the umbrella affair.

'Young Traill wants kicking,' he said. 'What are we all coming to, I should like to know? Why, the man 's only been here a month or two, and he goes and takes a senior master's things without asking leave, and then knocks him down because he objects. I never heard anything like it. The fellow wants kicking out altogether.'

Mrs. Comber said nothing.

'Well, why don't you say something? You 've got some opinion about it, I suppose; and there 's more in it than that—he 's gone and got himself engaged to Isabel, I hear. What 's the girl thinking of? They 're both much too young, anyhow. It 's absurd. I 'll tell her what I think of it.'

'Oh no, Freddie—don't say anything to her. She 's so happy about it, and I 'm sure the dear girl has been so good to both of us that she deserves some happiness, and I do want them to be successful. After all, if Mr. Traill was a little hasty, he 's very young, and Mr. Perrin 's a very difficult man to get on with. You know, dear, you 've always said——'

'Well, whatever I 've said,' he broke in furiously, 'I 've never advocated stealing nor hitting your elders and betters in the face, and if you think I have, you 're mightily mistaken.'

After that there was silence during the rest of the meal. Miss Desart was dining at the Squire's in the village, and, for once, Mrs. Comber was glad that the girl was not with them.

She was very near to tears. The day had been a most terrible one—and her food choked her. The meal seemed to stretch into infinity, the dreary dining-room, the monotonous tick of the clock, and always her husband's scowling face.

At last it was over, and he went to his study, and she to her little drawing-room. In front of her fire, her sewing slipped from her lap and she slept, with her purple dress shining in the firelight, and the rest of the room in shadow about her. And she dreamt wonderful dreams—of places where there was freedom and light, of hard, white roads and forests and cathedrals, and of a wonderful life where there was no travail nor ill-temper; and her face became happy again, and she saw Freddie as he had once been, before the shadow of this place had fallen about him, and in her dreams she was in a place where every one loved her and she could make no mistakes.

Then she woke up and saw Freddie Comber

standing near her, and she smiled at him and then gave a little exclamation because the fire was nearly out.

'Yes,' he said, following her glance, 'it 's a nice, cheerful room for a man to come into, isn't it, after he 's tired and cold with work? I have got a nice, pleasant little wife. I 'm a lucky man, I am.'

Then, as she began to busy herself with the fire, and tried to brighten it, he said, 'Oh, leave it now, can't you? What 's the use of making a noise and fuss with it now?'

Then he went on as she got up from her knees again and faced him, 'Look here, we 've got to come to an understanding about this business.'

'What business?' she said faintly, all the colour leaving her cheeks.

'Why, young Traill,' he went on, standing over her. 'I 'm not going to have my wife encouraging him in this affair. I tell you I object to him—he 's a conceited, impertinent prig, and he wants putting in his place, and I 'll let him know it if he comes near here. I won't have him in the house, and it 's just as well he should know it. So don't go asking him here.'

She was now white to the lips. 'But,' she said, 'I have told Isabel that I am glad, and I *am* glad. I like Mr. Traill, and I don't think it was his fault in this business; and, Freddie dear, you know you are not quite fair to him because of his football, or something silly, and I 'm sure you don't mind him, really—you don't like Mr. Perrin, you know.'

This was quite the most unfortunate speech that poor Mrs. Comber could possibly have made; the mention of the football at once reminded Freddie Comber of all that he had suffered on that head, and his neck began to swell with rage, and his cheeks were flushed.

'Look here, my lady,' he said, 'you just leave things alone that don't belong to you. Never you mind what reasons I 've got for disliking young Traill—it 's enough if I say that he 's not to come here—and Miss Isabel shall hear that from my own lips.'

In all her long experience of him she had never known him so angry as he was now, and she had never before been so afraid of him; but at the mention of Isabel, she called all her courage to her aid and drew herself up.

'You must not do that,' she said. 'You cannot insult Isabel here, when she has been such a friend of ours, and been so good—so good. I love her, and the man she is going to marry is my friend.'

'Oh!' he said, speaking very low and coming very close to her. 'This is defiance, is it? You will do this and that, will you? I tell you that he shall not come here.'

'And I say that he shall,' she answered in a whisper.

Then, with the accumulated irritation of the

day upon him, he suddenly came to her and, muttering between his teeth, 'We 'll see about the master here,' struck her so that he cut his hand on her brooch, and she fell back against the wall, and stayed there with her hands spread out against it, staring at him. . . .

There was a long silence, with no sound save the clock and the distant wind. He had never, in their long married life, struck her before. They both knew, as they stood there staring at one another, that a period had suddenly been placed, like an iron wall, in their lives. Their relations could never be the same again. They might be better, they might be worse—they could never be the same.

But with him there was a great overwhelming horror of what he had done. Her white face, her large, shining eyes, the way that her hands lay against the wall, and the way that her dress fell about her feet, because her knees were bending under her—drove this home to him. He was appalled; suddenly that man in him that had been dead for twenty years was brought to life by that blow.

'My dear—my dear—don't look at me like that—I did not mean anything—I am not angry—I am terribly ashamed. . . . Please——'

His voice was a trembling whisper. He put out his hand towards her. She took his hand, and came away from the wall, still looking at him fixedly.

'You never struck me before, Freddie,' she said. 'At least, you have never done that. I am so sorry, my dear.'

Then, very quietly, she put her arms about his neck and kissed him; then she went slowly out of the room.

He stood where she had left him motionless. Then he said, still in a whisper and looking at the curtains that hid the night and the dark buildings, 'Curse the place! It is that—it has done for me. . . .' And then, as he very slowly sat down and faced the fire, he whispered to the shadowy room, 'I am no good—I am no good at all!'

CHAPTER X

THE BATTLE OF THE UMBRELLA: 'WHOM THE GODS WISH TO DESTROY . . .'

I

DURING the month that followed, the battle raged furiously, and within a week of that original incident there was no one in the establishment who had not his or her especial grievance against someone else. In the Senior common room, at the middle morning hour, the whole staff might be seen, silent, grave, bending with sheer resolution over the daily papers, eloquent backs turned to their enemies, every now and again abstract sarcasm designed for some very concrete resting-place.

That original umbrella had, long ago, been forgotten, or, rather, the original borrowing of it. It had now become a flag, a banner—something that stood for any kind of principle that it might serve one's purpose to support. One hated one's neighbour—well, let any small detail be the provocation, the battle was the thing.

Imagine moreover the effect on the young generation, assembled to watch and imitate the thoughts and actions of their elders and betters;

what a delightful and admirable system!—with their Greek accents and verbs in '$\mu\iota$,' with their principal parts of *savoir* and *dire* and their conclusive decisions concerning vulgar fractions and the imports and exports of Sardinia, they should learn the delicate art of cutting your neighbour, of hating your fellow-creatures, of malicious misconception—all this within so small an area of ground, so slight a period of time, at so wonderfully inconsiderable an expense.

The question at issue speedily passed of course to the very smallest boy in the school, but here there was not so intense a division—there was indeed scarcely a division at all, because there could not, on the whole, be two opinions about it. When it came to choosing between Old Pompous with his stupid manners and his uncertain temper, with all the custom of his twenty years' stay at the school so that he was simply a tiresome tradition that present fathers of grown families had once accepted as a fearful authority—between this and the novel and athletic Traill with his splendid football and his easy fellowship . . . why! there was nothing more to be said. Why shouldn't one take Old Pompous's umbrella? Who was he to be so particular about his property? He wouldn't hesitate to take someone else's things if he wanted them. . . . Meanwhile there was an encouragement to rebellion amongst all those who came beneath his discipline—as to the way that he took this, there is more to be said later.

But the point about this month is not the question of individual quarrel and disturbance. Of that there was enough, and to spare, but there was nothing extraordinary about its progress, and every successive term saw something of the kind: the two questions as to whether Traill should have taken Perrin's umbrella and whether Isabel Desart should, under the circumstances, have allowed herself to be engaged to Traill, simply took the place of other questions that had, in their time, served to rouse combat. No—the peculiar fact about this month was that at the end of it, when their quarrels and hatreds should have reached their climax, they were sunk suddenly almost to the point of disappearance—they were almost lost and forgotten—and the reason of this was that every one in the place, in some cases unconsciously and in nearly every instance silently, was watching Perrin. . . . It had become during that time an issue between two men, and one of those men was passive. It was being worked out in silence—even the spectators themselves made no comment, but Mrs. Comber afterwards put it into words when she said that 'Every one was so afraid that talking about it might make it happen that no one said anything at all'—and that indeed was the remarkable fact.

Amongst all the eyes that were turned on the developing incident those most fitted for our purpose of elucidation belonged to Isabel Desart, and her experience of it all will do very well for every one else's experience of it, because the only difference between herself and the rest was that she was more acute in her judgment and had a more discerning intuition.

In the first place she had very crucially indeed to fight her own battles. It did not take her a day to discover that every lady in the place, with the single exception of Mrs. Comber, was, for the time being at any rate, up in arms against her. She ought not to have allowed herself to be engaged to Mr. Traill — there were no two opinions about it. It was not ladylike—she was allying herself to disorder and tumult, she was encouraging the stealing of things, and the knocking down of persons in authority—above all, she was setting herself up, whatever that might mean; all this was foreshadowed on that very first day in Mrs. Comber's drawing-room.

These things did not, in the very least, surprise or dismay Isabel. She loved a battle—she had never realized before how dearly she loved it, she gave no quarter and she asked none. She went about with her head up and her eyes flashing fire—she was quiet unless she was attacked; but so soon as there were signs of the enemy, the armour would be buckled on and the trumpet sounded. In a way—and it seemed to her curious when she looked back upon it—this month of hers was stirring and even rather delightful.

But there were other and more serious sides to

it. She saw at once that something had happened in the Comber family, and with all the tenderness and gentleness that was so wonderfully hers she sought to put it right. But she soon realized that it had all gone far too deep for any outside help. She did not know what had occurred on that evening when she had dined at the Squire's. Mrs. Comber told her nothing—she only begged her not to speak to Freddie about the umbrella quarrel and not to attempt to bring Archie to the house, at present at any rate.

But Mrs. Comber was now a different person—her animated volubility had disappeared altogether, she went about her house very quietly with a pale face and tired eyes, and she did not speak unless she was spoken to. But the change in Freddie Comber was still more marked. Isabel had never liked him so much before. His harsh dogmatism seemed to have disappeared. He said very little to anybody, but in his own house at any rate he was quiet, reserved, and even submissive. Isabel noticed that he was on the watch to do things for his wife, and sometimes she saw that his eyes would leave his work and stray about the room as though he were searching for something. He scarcely seemed to notice her at all, and sometimes when she spoke to him he would start and look at her curiously, almost suspiciously, as though he were wondering how much she knew. He was not kind and attentive to her, as he had been before—she felt sure that he had now a great dislike for her. All this made her miserable, and she loved to wonder sometimes what it was that held her back from speaking to Mrs. Comber about it all—but something prevented her.

The masters, she knew, were divided about her. They were, she thought, more occupied with their own quarrels and disputes than with any attitude towards herself. At first she was amused by their divided camps—it all seemed so childish and absurd, and for its very childishness it could not have a serious conclusion; but as the days went on and she saw into it all more deeply, the pathos of it caught her heart and she could have cried to think of what men they might have been, of the things that they might have done. Some of them seemed to seek her out now with a courtliness and deference that they had never shown her before. Birkland, of whom she had always been rather frightened, spoke to her now whenever there was an opportunity, and his sharp, sarcastic eyes softened, and she saw the sadness in their grey depths, and she felt in the pressure of his hands that he wanted now to be friends with her. White, too, was different now. He said very little to her, and he was so quiet that for him to speak at all was a wonderful thing, but there were a few words about his affection for Archie.

With all of this Isabel got a profound sense of its being her duty to do something; as far as her own affairs were concerned she was perfectly able to manage them, and if the matter in dispute had been simply her engagement to Archie, there would be no difficulty—it was a case of waiting, and then escaping; but things were more serious than that—something was in the air, and she knew enough of that life and that atmosphere to be afraid. But it was not until later than this that she began to be afraid definitely of Mr. Perrin.

But this feeling that she had of the necessity of doing something grew when she perceived the inertia of the others—inertia was perhaps scarcely the word: it was rather, as the matter advanced, an increasing impulse to sink their own quarrels and sit back in their chairs and wait for the result.

And, with this before her, Isabel set out on a determined campaign, having for its ultimate issue the hope of possible reconciliation—she could not put it more optimistically than that—before the end of the term came.

It was not at all a desire to do good that drove her — indeed, her flashing disputes with Mrs. Dormer, her skirmishes with the younger Miss Madder, were very far away from any evangelistic principles whatever—but rather some hint of future trouble that was hard to explain. She wished to prevent things happening, was the way that she herself would have put it; but that did not hinder her from feeling a natural anxiety that Miss Madder, Mrs. Dormer, and the rest should have some of their own shots back before the end of the term was reached.

II

But she began her campaign with her own Archie and found him difficult. Going down the hill by the village on one of those sharp, tightly drawn days with the horizon set like marble and nothing moving save the brittle leaves blowing like brown ghosts up and down, she tried to get him to see the difficulties as she saw them. She attacked him at first on the question of making peace with Mr. Perrin, and came up at once against a bristling host of obstinacies and traditions that her ignorance of public school and university laws had formerly hidden from her.

Perrin was a bounder, and young Traill's eyes were cold and hard as he summed it all up in this sentence. He would do anything in the world for Isabel, but she didn't probably altogether understand what a fellow felt—there were things a man couldn't do. She found that the laws of the Medes and Persians were nothing at all in comparison with the stone tables of public school custom: 'The man was a bounder'—'There were things a fellow couldn't do.'

She had not expected him to go and beg for peace—she had not probably altogether wished him to; but the way that he looked at it all left her with a curious mixture of feelings: she felt that he was so immensely young, and therefore to be—most delightful of duties—looked after.

Also she felt, for the first time, all the purpose and obstinacy of his nature, so that she foresaw that there would in the future between them be a great many tussles and battles.

But she was very much cleverer than he was, and dealt with him gently, and then suddenly gave him a sharp little moral rap, and then kissed him afterwards. She found, in fact, that this trouble with Mr. Perrin was worrying him dreadfully. He hid it as well as he could, and hid it on the whole successfully; but Isabel dragged it all out and saw that he hated quarrelling with anybody, and that he now dimly discovered that he was the centre of a vulgar dispute and that people were taking sides about him — all this was horrible.

He also felt very strongly the injustice of it. 'I never meant to knock the fellow down. I never knew I'd taken his beastly umbrella—all this fuss!'—which was, Isabel thought, so very like a man, because the thing was done and there was no more to be said about it. He thought a great deal about her in the matter and was very anxious to stand up for her; indeed, that was the only aspect of the affair that gave him any satisfaction—that they should be fighting shoulder to shoulder against the 'low, bounding' world, and he declared, as he looked at her, that he loved her more and more every day.

But all this did not touch on his relations with Perrin, and his eyes with regard to that gentleman could only look one way—he would not make advances.

The more Isabel felt his determination, the more, curiously enough, she felt Mr. Perrin's pathos. She had not yet arrived at that definite watching of him that was to come upon them all soon so strangely; but when she thought of him she thought of Archie's definition of him, and she realized, as she had not realized before, that that would be a great many other persons' definition of him also. Whatever he was—cross, irritable, violent, even wicked—he was, at any rate, lonely, and that was enough to make Isabel sorry, and more than sorry.

She could not, of course, make Archie see that. 'The fellow 's always wanted to be lonely—thinks himself much too good for other people's society, that's the fact, and if a man behaves like a beast, he must expect to be left alone.'

That did not worry Archie. The whole of his annoyance arose from the fact that there should be such a fuss. He had never really quarrelled with any one before—people *never* did quarrel with him; and now suddenly here were Comber and West and the little French worm Pons, stiff and sulky whenever they met him, and Moy-Thompson bullying him whenever he got the opportunity.

Of course he wasn't going to stay! he couldn't stay under these circumstances—but it was all unpleasant and disagreeable. Isabel herself was only too anxious to take him out of it all as soon as possible. He wasn't wearing well under it. He had been full of light and sunshine at the beginning of the term, pleasant to every one, equable, comfortable, a splendid creature to be with. Now the boys of his class found that nothing pleased him, little things roused him to a fury, and he snapped at people when they spoke to him. With Isabel he was always gentle, but his eager eyes were tired, and once he wasn't very far away from tears.

But she did not allow any of these things to worry her. She was proud with Miss Madder, haughty with Mrs. Moy-Thompson, gentle with Mrs. Comber, always amusing and cheerful with Archie. But when she had gone to bed and was at last alone, she would lie there, trying to puzzle it all out, afraid of what the future might bring, and praying that she might drag Archie out of it all before they had damaged him. He was such a boy, and all this discussion was so new to him; but she felt that she herself was ninety at least, and she would wonder sometimes that all men's difficult education seemed to leave them just where they began, which was several stages earlier than the place where women commenced. Love and death were very simple things, it seemed to her, beside the tangled daily worries of people getting along together. Her present feeling was something akin to Alice's sensation at the Croquet party when the mallets (being flamingoes) would walk away and climb up trees, and the balls (being hedgehogs) would wander off the ground. They were all flamingoes and hedgehogs at Moffatt's.

III

But towards the end of this month, Isabel became suddenly conscious of Mr. Perrin in a very different way. It was now only three weeks before the end of term, and in another week examinations would begin. That something in the atmosphere that signified the coming of examinations was busy about the place. People were very quiet, and then suddenly in the most singular way would break out; there was continual quarrel in the common room, strange rumours were carried of things that people had said—it was all a question of strain.

There came, it now being the first week in December, the first day of snow, and the light feathery flakes fell throughout the afternoon, and when the sun set there was a soft, white world with the buildings black and grim and a sky of hurrying grey cloud. Isabel and Mrs. Comber sat in Mrs. Comber's little drawing-room over a roaring fire, and there was no other light in the room.

Mrs. Comber sat, as she so often sat now, with her chin resting in her hand, silently staring at the fire.

Isabel was unhappy; the silent whiteness of

the world outside, the consciousness of Miss Madder's rudeness to her that afternoon, the trouble that she had seen in Archie's eyes when she had said good night to him after chapel, above all a general sense of strain and nerves stretched to breaking-point—all this overwhelmed her. She had never felt so strongly before that she and Archie, if they were to keep anything at all of their vitality, must escape at once . . . to-night . . . to-morrow; it might be too late.

She knew that Archie had lost his temper with West that afternoon, that he had called him 'a rotten little counter-jumper,' and that West had made an allusion to 'stealing things.' Where were they all? What were they all doing to be fighting like this?

They sat in silence opposite to one another, one on each side of the fire, and the ticking of the clock, and every now and again a tumbling coal, were the only sounds. Then suddenly Isabel broke out.

'Oh! I can't stand it any longer; I feel as though I should go mad. What is the matter with everybody? Why are we all fighting like this? Oh! I *do* want to be pleasant to somebody again, just for a change. For the last three weeks, ever since that wretched quarrel, there has been no peace at all.'

'I know,' Mrs. Comber answered without raising her eyes from the fire; 'I am very tired, too, and it 's a good thing there are only three weeks more of the term, because I 'm sure that somebody would be cutting somebody's throat if it lasted any longer, and I wouldn't mind very much if somebody would cut mine.' She gave a little choke in her throat, and then suddenly her head fell forward into her hands, and she burst into passionate sobbing.

Isabel said nothing, but came over to her and knelt down by her chair and took her other hand. They stayed together in silence for a long time, and the burning fire flung great shadows on the walls, and the snow had begun to fall again and rustled very softly and gently against the window.

At last Mrs. Comber looked up and wiped her eyes, and tried to smile.

'Ah! my dear, you are so good to me. I don't know what I should have done this terrible term if you hadn't been here—and now my eyes are a perfect sight, and Freddie will be coming in; but I couldn't help it. Things only seem to get worse and worse and worse, and I 've stood it as long as I can, and I can't stand it any longer. I think I shall go away and be a nun or a hospital nurse or something where you 're let alone.'

'Dear Mrs. Comber,' said Isabel, still holding her hand, 'do tell me about these last few weeks, if it would help you. Of course, I 've seen that something 's happened between you and Mr. Comber. I can see that he is most dreadfully sorry about something, and I know that he wants to make it up. But this silence is worse than anything, and if you 'd only have it out, both of you, I 'm sure it would get all right.'

'No, dear.' Mrs. Comber shook her head and wiped her eyes. 'It 's not that so much. Freddie and I will get all right again, I expect, and even be better together than we were before; but all this business has shown me, my dear, that I 'm a failure. I 've known it really all the time, and I used to pretend that if one was nice enough to people one couldn't be altogether a failure, because they wanted one to like one—and that 's the truth. Nobody wants me to like them, and I 'm the loneliest woman in the world. I 'm not grumbling about it, because I suppose I 'm careless and silly and untidy, but I don't think any one 's wanted friends quite so badly as I have, and some people have such a lot. I used to think it was all just accidents, but now I know it 's really me; and now you 're going to be married there 's an end of you, the only person I had.'

'Archie and I,' said Isabel softly, 'will care for you to the end of your days, and you will come and stay with us, won't you? And you know that Freddie loves you. Why, I 've seen him looking at you during these last weeks as though he could die for you, and then he 's been afraid to say anything. It 's only this horrid place that has got in the way so dreadfully.'

Mrs. Comber caught her hand eagerly. 'Do you really think so, my dear? Oh! if I could only think that, because I have fancied he 's been different lately, and he 's such a dear when he likes to be and isn't worried about his form; but things are always worse at examination time, and I always pray that the two weeks may be got through as quickly as possible; and something *dreadful did* happen the other day, and I know he was ashamed of himself, the poor dear. . . . Perhaps things will be all right.'

Mrs. Comber gave a great sigh and looked a little more cheerful. Then, after a pause, she began again, but a little doubtfully: 'You know, Isabel dear, there 's something else. I don't want to frighten you, but Mrs. Dormer noticed it as well, and I know it 's really silly of me, but I don't quite like it——'

'Like what?' said Isabel.

'Well, Mr. Perrin; he 's been looking so queer ever since that quarrel with your Archie. I dare say you haven't noticed anything, and I dare say it may be all my own imaginations, and I 'm sure in a place like this one might imagine anything——'

'How does he look queer?' said Isabel quietly.

'Well, it 's his eyes, I suppose, and the things the boys say about him. You know, my dear, I 've wondered since whether perhaps he didn't care about you rather a great deal, and whether that isn't another reason for his disliking Archie—'

'Care about me?' said Isabel, laughing; 'why, no, of course not. He 's only spoken to me once or twice.'

'Well,' said Mrs. Comber, 'I 've seen him looking at you in the strangest way in chapel. And his face has got so white and thin and drawn, I 'm really quite sorry for the poor man. And his eyes are so odd, as though he was trying to see something that wasn't there. And the boys say that he 's so strange in class sometimes and stops suddenly in the middle of a lesson and forgets where he is; and Mr. Clinton was telling me that he never speaks to Archie, but sometimes when Archie 's there he gets very white and shakes all over and leaves the room. I only want you to warn Archie to be careful, because when a man 's lonely like that and begins to think about things, he might do anything.'

'Why, what could he do?' Isabel said, with a little catch in her breath.

'Well, I don't know, dear,' Mrs. Comber said rather uncertainly. 'Only when examinations come on they do seem to get into the men's heads so, and it 's only that I thought that Archie might be careful and ready if Mr. Perrin seemed odd at all. . . .'

Mrs. Comber left it all very uncertain, and as they sat silently in the room with the fire turning from a roaring blaze into a golden cavern and the shadows on the wall growing smaller and smaller as the fire fell, Isabel seemed to feel the cold black and white of the world outside gather ominously about her.

She said good night very quietly, and the two

women clung to each other a moment longer than usual, as though they did not wish to leave each other.

'At any rate,' said Isabel, 'whatever else this place may do, it can't alter our being together. You 've always got me, you know.'

But from this moment Isabel was afraid. Perhaps her nerves were strained, perhaps she saw a great deal more than there was to be seen; but she longed for the end of the term with a passionate eagerness, and she could not sleep at nights.

And then, curiously, on the very next morning Mr. Perrin came and spoke to her.

She always afterwards remembered him as she saw him that day. She was just turning out of the black gate to go down the hill to the village; there was a pale blue sky; the ground was white with grey and purple shadows, and the houses were brown and sharply edged, as though cut out of paper, in the distance; the hills were a grey-white against the sky. He came towards her very slowly, and she saw that he wanted to speak to her, so she stopped and waited for him. When he came up to her—with his gown hanging loosely about him, and his heavy, black mortar-board, with his thin, haggard cheeks, and staring eyes, with his straggly, unkempt moustache—she had a moment of ungovernable fear. She could give no reason for it, but she knew that her impulse was to turn and run away, anywhere so that she might escape from him.

Then she controlled herself and turned and faced him, and smiled and held out her hand.

She could see him staring beyond her, over her shoulder, with eyes that didn't see her at all. She saw that his hand was shaking.

'How do you do, Mr. Perrin? I haven't seen you for quite a long time. Isn't this snow delightful? If it will only stay like this . . .'

Suddenly he came quite close to her, looking into her eyes; he grasped her hand and held it.

'I 've been wanting to say . . .' he said in an odd voice, and there he stopped and stood staring at her.

'Yes,' she said gently.

His throat was moving convulsively, and he put his hand up to his face with a helpless gesture and pulled his moustache.

'I 've wanted to say—um, ah—to congratulate you . . .'

He cleared his throat, and suddenly she saw tears in his eyes.

'Oh! thank you!' she said impulsively, coming up to him and putting her hand on his arm. 'Thank you so very much!' And then she could say no more.

He moved his arm away, and his eyes passed her again, out to the distant horizon. Then he said very rapidly, as though he were reciting a speech that he had learnt, 'I wanted to congratulate you on your engagement. I hope you 'll be very happy. I 'm sure you will. I 'm afraid

I 'm a little late in my good wishes. I 'm afraid I 'm a little late. Yes. Good morning!'

Then, before she could say any more, he had moved away and gone down the path.

As she watched his black gown waving a little behind him she knew that her vague fears of the night before had taken definite form.

CHAPTER XI

MR. PERRIN SEES DOUBLE

I

MEANWHILE, many things had happened to Mr. Perrin during this month. On that night after Clinton had told him about Miss Desart's engagement to Traill, he did not go to bed for many hours, but sat over his black grate without moving until the morning. He did not know until this had happened to him how greatly he had valued his dreams. To every man in middle life there comes a day when he sees clearly and pitilessly that he has missed his ambitions, or, if he has gained them, that there were other ambitions that would have been more profitable of pursuit; and then, if the rest of his days are to be worthily and honourably spent, he must make reckoning with other things that have perhaps no glitter nor promise, but will give him enough—life has no compensation for cynics.

In that black night, the darkest night of his life, Perrin saw that his last claim to that chance to which he had clung from his earliest boyhood was gone. At first, in the blind pathos of his disappointment, it seemed to him that she had promised to marry him and had left him at the altar. A great wave of self-pity swept over him, and he sat with his head in his hands, and the tears trickled through his thin fingers. The things that he could have done had she been faithful to him!—that was the way he put it. He saw now scenes that had occurred between them. He had pleaded his love, and she had accepted him; her head had rested on his breast, and, in that very room, he had held her and kissed her and stroked her hair.

And then, slowly as the room grew colder and the faint grey dawn came in at the window, he knew that that was not true; she had never cared about him, she had scarcely spoken to him; how could she care for a man like him—that sort of creature?

What had God meant by making a man like that? It was His game, perhaps; it pleased Him perhaps to have some ridiculous animal there that other men might sport with it—other beardless boys like Traill. . . .

He felt that he would like to take his revenge on God. He would show God that he was not the kind of man to be played with like that—he would mock at Him and show that he didn't care, that he was not afraid—ah! but he *was* afraid, terribly afraid. He had always been afraid, since those days when, a very small boy in short trousers, he had sat listening to the clergyman who had painted pictures of hell with such lurid and wonderful accuracy.

God was like that—He took away from you all the things that made life worth living, and then punished you with eternal fire afterwards because you resented His behaviour.

Mr. Perrin was not crying now, because his head ached so badly that the pain of it prevented any tears. He was sitting with his eyes very large and bright and his cheeks very white and drawn. When his head ached, it always meant that that other Mr. Perrin whose appearances he had now so long attempted to control came creeping out—that other Mr. Perrin who did not want him to have his chance, that other Mr. Perrin whom he did not want his friends to see.

On this night for the first time in his life that other Mr. Perrin seemed to have a concrete appearance and form. He was standing, Mr. Perrin fancied, somewhere in the corner of the room, and he was watching. He was wearing the same clothes, and he had the same features, but it was an evil face—all the eyes and nose and mouth and ears had gone wrong. Mr. Perrin had kept him in control so long; but now at last he had broken out, and perhaps he would never go away again.

Mr. Perrin was dreadfully afraid that he had come to stay.

Then, as the minutes passed, Mr. Perrin was conscious that there was something that this other Mr. Perrin wanted him to do. It had some connection with that young Traill. Mr. Perrin was conscious that now, as he thought of him, he had no anger in his brain about young Traill. No, there was nothing to be angry about—of course not—no; but he knew that there was something that the other Mr. Perrin thought that he ought to do to young Traill. What was it?

Then, very slowly, as though he were awaking out of a bad dream, Mr. Perrin pulled himself together. That other Mr. Perrin passed from the room, and the cold grey dawn crept across the floor. He was very desolate and very unhappy. He thought perhaps he would kill himself, and so end it all. What did people do? They hung themselves, or they shot themselves, or they poisoned themselves. No, he knew that he would be afraid to do any of those things. He was afraid of the pain and also, in an inconsequent way, of the sight that he would look afterwards.

There came to him the curious, strange idea that perhaps this was his great chance—the chance that he had been waiting for all his life. Perhaps God intended to knock him down as far as He could, so as to give him the opportunity of rising. Supposing he rose now, supposing he showed them that he did not care about Miss Desart or young Traill, supposing he won a fine position and did magnificently . . . but then, of course, it was absurd; after twenty years in Moffatt's one did not 'do' magnificently anywhere.

No, he was no good—he was done for. He thought, as he heard the clock strike five, he would go to bed. And then he lay there, staring at the yellow flowers on the wall-paper. There were five in a row, and then four, and then three, and then two, and then five again. . . . They were ugly flowers. He wanted Miss Desart! he wanted Miss Desart! he wanted Miss Desart! He bit the pillow and lay with his face buried in it, his thin, sharp shoulders heaving. . . . He wanted Miss Desart! . . .

His misery came upon him now in great clouds, and it buffeted him and enveloped him, and left him at last weak and shaking.

Young Traill had done this—young Traill was his enemy . . . young Traill! He hated him, and would do him harm if he could. . . .

And then, across the grey floor, outlined against the yellow paper flowers, he saw once more the grey figure of the other Mr. Perrin.

II

But when the morning came, and as the days passed, he found that it all resolved itself into an effort to keep control. This was very hard. When he had been a small boy there had been a picture that used to hang in his mother's dining-room. It was a grey picture of a skeleton that sat with a grin on its ghastly face on a huge iron chest studded with great black nails. The lid was raised a little, and from under it peeped the eyes of some wretched man, and over the edge there hung a grasping, wrenching hand. Someone was in there, someone was trying to get out, and the skeleton was sitting on the box. . . .

It was like that now with Mr. Perrin; there was something in him that was trying to get out, and he was determined that it should not. He found at once that he could not bear to be in the same room with Traill, and as the days advanced this feeling did not decrease. The feeling inside him that he must not let out was always stronger and more violent when Traill was there. Of course they did not speak to one another, but it was something more active than mere silent avoidance. They had struggled on the floor together, struggled before Comber and Birkland—Perrin would not forget that. He remembered it as an act of faith and said it to himself a great many times. He always found that when he was in the room with Traill something seemed to drag him across the floor towards him, and he had to hold himself back.

This was all very difficult, and he found it very hard to keep his mind on his form. It was more necessary than ever to keep his mind on his form, because he fancied that there was a new spirit abroad amongst them. They must, of course, have heard all about the quarrel, and he thought that when he was with them they laughed at him and mocked amongst themselves.

They had always done that, of course, but now there was an added reason.

There was one thing that they did at the Lower School that he always hated. When the bell rang at five minutes to one for luncheon, the master who was on duty was supposed to station himself at the door of the hall and look at the boys' hands, as the boys filed in, to see whether they were clean. Perrin had always hated doing this; it had seemed to him most undignified, and the sight of fifty pairs of hands raised to his eyes, one after the other—hands that were ill-kept, bitten, and ragged, and torn—this had been, in some hidden way, irritating. Now it was much more irritating, so that when it was his week on duty and this horde of boys passed him, raising their hands, as it seemed to him, with insolence and levity, he wanted to scream, to beat them all down, to run amok amongst them, to trample until all the hands were broken and bleeding.

Garden Minimus had often been turned back for having dirty hands. He used to try to slip through with the crowd, and Perrin had called him up, and he had come with a twinkling smile, and his hands had been very inky. Then Perrin, with apparent austerity, but in reality with a kindly eye, had sent him back to wash. But now the boy made no attempt to escape, but with a grave, serious face passed slowly along; his hands were always beautifully clean—he did not look at Perrin. This was, of course, a very small affair.

But afterwards, when they had all passed in, when they stood silently behind their forms and he began the Latin grace, and at the end 'per Jesum Christum Dominum nostrum' and a great clatter of forms being dragged out and people sitting down and the hum of voices—then he wanted to run amongst them and strike their stupid faces, but he knew that he must not.

One day at the very beginning he had suddenly found that he was alone in the Junior common room with Traill, and Traill had begun to speak to him.

Traill was standing away from him at the window and he scarcely turned his head, but over his shoulder in a gruff voice: 'I say, Perrin, isn't this rather rot, our quarrelling like this? I hate not to be speaking to a fellow—I 'm sorry if I did things, but you know——'

And Perrin, with his head a little lowered and his hands swinging, had moved towards him, making a curious little noise in his throat, and Traill had seen his face and stepped back against the window.

But Perrin had remembered that picture in his mother's dining-room. No! that man must not get out—he must at all costs be kept in his box. And so he had turned and left the room without saying anything.

Traill did not try to speak to him again.

With his form during these days Perrin was very quiet. It was remarked afterwards how quiet he had been. He was never angry. Boys did bad work, and he did not seem to mind, but he looked at them in a strange way and said, 'Go back, and do it again—do it again,' as though he were not thinking of what he said.

Perhaps he did not altogether realize them during those days, but rather thought of them as faces and boots. There were faces in a row, white faces, and then there was a long strip of wooden desk, scarred with ink, and then there were boots, broad-toed boots, sometimes with laces hanging down, stupid things like toads.

He had taught the things that he taught so often that it needed no effort now to think of them. When you began with numbers on the board, other numbers followed, and then an answer, and a face got five marks if it was right—that was all. He never spoke to Garden Minimus if he could help it. He did not analyse his silence—it was merely a fact that he did not wish to have Garden Minimus's face brought too close to his own . . . it reminded him of things that hurt.

But, on the whole, his form did not notice any delightful difference except that there was a visible slackening of authority. One could do things with pins and ink and other people's books more often than had hitherto been the case, and Pomfret-Walpole perhaps felt the difference more severely than any one else. . . . That was really all that there was to say about his form.

It was perhaps about a week after the Battle of the Umbrella broke out that Perrin noticed two things. The first thing that he noticed was that he saw Traill when Traill wasn't there. This was very odd and very provoking. It could not be said with real accuracy that he saw him, because he was always just round the corner and out of his eye. One morning during an Algebra hour, sitting at his desk, he suddenly felt that Traill was standing just inside the door. It was very odd of Traill to do this, because he ought, by rights, to have been teaching at the Upper School—moreover, the door had apparently made no sound when it opened, and none of the boys seemed to notice his entrance; also Mr. Perrin could not be quite sure, because he was not looking at the door at all but at the board in front of him. He knew exactly how Traill was standing, and at last his motionless silence was so irritating that he turned round sharply and looked at the door, but Traill was not there.

The silence that was between them, the elaborate prevention of conversation when they were together at meals or in a room, came slowly to Perrin as an added impertinence. He knew now that he hated Traill with all his heart and soul, but that was a very mild way of putting it. It was not hatred that he felt when he found

Traill's face opposite him at dinner; it was something more active than that. It was as though someone at his elbow was urging him to leap across the table, dragging the cloth with him as he went, and to catch Traill's throat . . . and to do things; but he knew that he must not, because something must be kept in a box. And the other thing that he noticed about this time was that people were talking about him. This might almost be called the Irritation of the Closed Door, because on every occasion that he saw a closed door—and they were very many—he knew that there were people behind it who were talking about him. Sometimes he suddenly opened, very softly, a door and looked, and although there was, as a rule, no one in the room, he was sure that they were hiding in cupboards and behind chairs. Once when he opened a door suddenly like that, the stout Miss Madder was alone in the room, sewing, and when she saw him she dropped her work and screamed, which was foolish of her.

But they were all of them always talking about him, and he would like to have heard what they said. He wondered what Miss Desart said—he was sure that she would be kind—and he stared at her very hard in chapel, because he saw her so very little at other times, and because he would like to know what she was thinking about. He would like to know whether it was about the same things as his things—and so he stared at her in a curious way.

And then one evening he suddenly discovered that it was the day on which he wrote to his mother. He had omitted to write to her last week for the first time for very many years, because he had forgotten, and she had written saying how much she had missed it; so he must not forget it again.

He had had a very trying day, and the man in the box had more nearly broken out than ever before, so that at first it was very hard to think of his mother at all. But he stood in the middle of the room with his hands to his throbbing head, and he made in his mind a little picture of her sitting in her lace cap and black gown, waiting for a letter from him. He sat down in his chair and lit his lamp and took out his pen and paper, and began, as he had begun for a great many years: 'Dear old Lady . . .'

Then suddenly he thought that Traill was in the room, standing, as he did now, just inside the door. He turned sharply in his chair, and held the lamp up towards the door, but there was no one there. He sat with his head between his hands and cleared his mind of everything except his mother; and gradually, as he sat there, all that strange state that had been about him during these days fell from him, and he regained his clear vision—he began to write as he always did:

'. . . I didn't write last week, because I had so much to do. I really didn't have time, and you know how busy we get during these days with the examinations coming on and everything.

'I 'm very well, except that I have these headaches—nothing at all, and I 'm taking these liver pills that you told me of. I hope you 're all right, and that Dr. Sandars comes to see you every week. Keeping warm 's the thing, old lady, with this weather, and that shawl that Miss Bennett gave you is the very thing—mind you wear it, and don't sit in draughts. I 'm all right. . . .'

And then the pen dropped from his fingers, and his head fell between his hands. He wanted to tell her about Miss Desart, that she needn't be afraid now of his marrying any one, that he was never going to marry. . . . His mind was very clear now. It was like a moor when the mists have lifted away from it. . . . His unhappiness came all about him and held him to the ground. He did not hate Traill—Traill could not help it; but he wanted her—oh! he wanted her so dreadfully.

He slipped on to his knees on the ground, and he was terribly troubled so that his back shook. He began with desperation, as though it were his last hold on life, to pray.

'O God, God, God! . . . Help me! . . . Do not let me go back again to that state that I have just been in. I cannot hold myself when I am like that. I do not know what I am doing or thinking. But it is all so hard—there are so many little things—there is no time! . . . They will not let me alone. . . . O God! give me my chance, give me my chance! Give me someone to love; I am so terribly alone . . . nobody wants me. O God! do not let me go back to that darkness again. . . . I am so afraid of what I may do. . . .'

But at last exhaustion took him, there on the floor, and he slept with his head on his arm.

And suddenly he awoke in the middle of the night and found himself there—and it was all very dark. He rose to his feet and was terribly frightened, because there, a grey figure against the fireplace, was the other Mr. Perrin—and he knew that God had not answered his prayer, and he cursed God and stumbled to his bed.

III

And after that, things, for him, developed in an amazing way. He was quite sure now that God hated him.

Now that he was sure of that, he need not care so much about keeping that box closed—he was damned anyhow.

Traill now took complete possession of his mind. He never thought of any one else, and it was exactly as though an iron weight was pressing on his head, shutting him down. He must get rid of that iron weight, because it was so disagreeable and prevented him thinking; but he was sure that it would not go until he had got rid of Traill; therefore Traill must go.

He did not know how Traill would be likely to go, but he began to consider it. . . .

These days before the examinations began were very difficult for everybody, and Perrin began that hideous 'getting behind-hand' that made things accumulate so that there seemed no chance of ever catching up. There were all the term's marks to be added up before the examinations began, there were trial papers and test questions to be set, and therefore a great many papers to be corrected. He found that he was not able to keep at it for very long at a time, but would sit in his chair with his hands folded in front of him and think of Traill; and then he would find that the papers were not corrected and that there were others to be done, and they would be in dingy piles about his room—sometimes a pile would slip from the table on to the floor and would lie there scattered, and he would feel his rage rising so that if he had not, with all his force, kept it down he would have rushed screaming about his room.

But with the whole staff this irritation was at work, and Perrin welcomed it because it amused him, and because it seemed to him in tune with his own moods. Always this week before the examinations was a very difficult one, but now, this term, it was worse than it had ever been before.

The place was badly understaffed, and always at this time the work was multiplied so that any spare hours that there had been before were now filled to overflowing. Also the examination scheme had now appeared, and, whether by design or not, Moy-Thompson always arranged it so that one or two men seemed to have scarcely any work at all, and the others naturally had a great deal more than they could do. The quarrels that had broken out over the umbrella incident had developed until there was very little to prevent physical struggle. It happened that on this occasion West was the person who was let off easily by the examination list, and he was not the kind of man to allow his advantage to pass without comment.

Perrin passed a considerable amount of time now in the Senior common room. He never talked to any one, but would sit in a dark corner by the window and watch them all. The funniest thoughts came to him as he sat there: for instance, he fancied that it would be pleasant, when they were not watching, to crawl under the table and bite White's legs—it would be amusing to spring suddenly from behind on to Comber's back, and to strip all the clothes from him until he was stark naked, and must run, screaming, from the room—or to twist Birkland's ears round and round until they were torn and hung. . . . All these things would be pleasant to do, but he sat in his corner and said nothing.

At last the day before the examinations arrived, and they were nearly all gathered in the Senior common room in the half-hour before chapel.

Perrin, with his white face and untidy hair, watched them from his corner.

'It will be very pleasant,' West said, smiling a little, 'to have that third hour off all through this week. I can't think, Comber, why Moy-Thompson's given you all that extra Latin to do—I——'

'For God's sake,' Comber broke out furiously, 'stop it! Aren't we all sick to death with hearing of your beastly good luck? Don't we all know that the whole thing 's about as unfair as it is possible for anything to be? Just keep quiet about it if you can.'

'Oh, of course, Comber,' said West. 'You grudge a man any bit of luck that he may have. It 's just like you. I never knew anything more selfish. If you 'd had an hour off yourself, you 'd have let us know about it all right.'

'Well, stop talking about it anyhow, West,' said Dormer. 'Leave it alone. Can't you see that we 're all as tired out as we can be? We 've had enough fighting this term to last us a century.'

With common consent they seemed to sink their private differences in a common thought of that strange, silent man sitting behind them. They all drew closer together. The pale gas-light fell on their faces, and they were all white and tired, with heavy, dark marks under their eyes.

With their dark gowns, their long white hands, their pale faces, their heavy eyes, they moved silently about the room and gathered at last in a cluster by the fire, and stood and sat silently without a word. Only Perrin, hidden in the shadow behind them, did not move.

Then suddenly Birkland, who was standing a little away from the rest with his back against the wall, spoke.

'You 're right, Dormer. We 've fought enough this term to fill a great many years. We 're a wretched enough crew.'

He paused; but no one spoke, and no one moved.

'I wonder sometimes,' he went on, 'how long we are going to stand it. Most of us have been here a great many years—most of us have had our hopes broken a great many years ago—most of us have lost our pluck——'

Perhaps he expected a vehement denial, because he paused; but no one spoke, and no one moved. 'This term has been worse than any other since I have been here. We have all been very near doing things as well as thinking them. I wonder if you others have ever thought, as I have thought sometimes, that we have no right to be here?'

'How do you mean,' said Comber slowly, 'no right?'

'Well, we were not always like this. We were not always fighting and cursing like beasts. We were not always without any decency or friendliness or kindliness. We did not always have a man over us who used us like slaves, because he knew that we were afraid to give him notice and go. I was a man myself once. I thought that I was going to do things—we all thought that we were going to do things. Look at the lot of us, now——'

He paused again, but there was still silence.

'They say to us—the people outside—that it is our own fault, that other men have made a fine thing of teaching, that there are fine schools where life is splendid, that we have the interests of the boys under us in our hands. I know that—we all know that there are splendid schools and splendid lives; but what has that to do with us? . . . Do they know the kind of man that we have got over us? Do they know that every time that we have tried to do decently, it has been crushed out of us by that devil? Not a minute is our own, even in the holidays we are pursued. Let others come and try and see what they will make of it.'

A little stir like a wind passed through the listeners, but no one spoke. Birkland was leaning forward; his eyes were on fire, his hands waving in the air.

'But it is not too late—it is not too late, I tell you. Let us break from it, let us go for the governors in a body and tell them that unless they improve our conditions, unless they remove Moy-Thompson, unless they give us more freedom, we will leave—in a body. There is a chance if we can act together, and better, far better, that we break stones in the road, that we die free men than this . . . that this should go on.'

His voice was almost a shout. 'My God!' he cried, 'think of it! Think of our chance! We are not dead yet. There is time. Let us act together and break free!—free!'

He had caught them, he had held them. They saw with his eyes. They moved together. Cries broke from them.

'You 're right, Birkland; you 're right. We won't stand it. It 's our last chance.'

'Now! Let us go now!'

'Let us go and face him!'

Suddenly the door opened. Into the midst of their noise there came the voice of the school-sergeant, cold, unmoved—the voice of a thousand years of authority: 'The head master would like to see Mr. White as soon as possible.'

It was the test. They all realized it as they turned to White to see what he would do.

For a moment he stood there, tall, gaunt, haggard, his eyes held by Birkland's, the fire dying from them. For a moment he seemed to hesitate, his lips moved as though he would speak—then, with a helpless gesture of his hand, he moved slowly, with hanging head, down the room, and passed out through the door.

There was silence, and then from his chair in the dark corner Perrin laughed.

CHAPTER XII

MR. PERRIN WALKS IN HIS SLEEP

I

WITH examinations there comes a new element into the life of the term—it is an element of triumph in so far as it marks the approaching end of an impossible situation; it is an element of despair in so far as it provides an overpowering number of answers, differing in the minutest particulars, to the same questions; and is even an element of romance, because it heralds the appearance of a final order in which boys will beat other boys, generally in a surprising and unforeseen manner. But whatever it means it also tightens to a higher pitch any situation that there may have been before, so that anything that seemed impossible now appears incredible; the days are like years, and the hours, filled with the empty scratching of pens and the rubbing of blotting-paper, stretch infinitely into the distance and hide release.

Their effect on every one on the present occasion was to force extravagantly the longing that everything might soon be over, that the situation couldn't stand the kind of strain that was being put upon it unless the curtain were rung down as soon as possible. Every one was hideously busy with long periods of doing nothing except the aforesaid attention to pens and blotting-paper. Mr. Moy-Thompson had, moreover, invented a little scheme which always provided, as far as he was concerned, the pleasantest and most happy results. This was a plan whereby every master set and corrected the papers of some other master's form and then wrote a report on them. Here obviously was a most admirable opportunity for the paying off of old scores, as a bad report always led, next term, to a miserable period of bullying and baiting, with the hapless master who had incurred it in the role of victim. Therefore, if, as was usually the case, your especial enemy was correcting the papers of your form and would write a report on them, unless something were done to appease him, you were, during the whole of the next term, delivered over mercilessly to the Rev. Moy-Thompson. You might perchance appease your enemy, or you might yourself be examining *his* form, in which case you had every opportunity of a pleasant retort. At any rate, this plan invariably inflamed any hostilities that might already be in existence and resulted in the provision of at least half a dozen victims for Mr. Moy-Thompson's games on a later occasion.

For once, however, these examinations came to Perrin as very vague and misty affairs. This was not usual with him. As a rule they pleased him, because he could hold over boys who had been rude to him during the term the terror of being detained all the first day of the holidays—also he considered that he was ingenious in the invention of pleasant Algebraic conundrums and fascinating, derisive questions in Trigonometry that prevented any possible solution. The devising of these gave him, as a rule, pleasure and amusement, but this term he could not face them.

He set his papers, in an odd, abstracted way, with questions from earlier papers, and then he sat with his hands folded in front of him and waited. There was only one subject now in the whole world, and all these curious boys, these strange, visionary class-rooms, these appalling noises, and then these equally appalling silences, only diverted his attention and prevented his thinking.

There were always three of them now—himself, the other Mr. Perrin, and Traill—they always went about together. When he was taking an examination and was sitting at his desk, isolated, by the wall, the other Mr. Perrin, a grey, thin figure, was behind him, looking into the room, and Traill stood, as he always did now, just inside the door, but away from Mr. Perrin's eye, because when he turned round and looked at him he always slipped, in the cleverest way, out of the door.

Perrin wondered that other people didn't

notice that he was accompanied by these persons, but probably they were all too deeply occupied with their own affairs. Of course Traill must be got rid of—one couldn't possibly have any one whom one hated as much as that always with one. Sometimes it was curiously confused, because there were two Traills — a Traill who moved about and spoke to people (although never to Perrin), and the Traill who stood always by the door and never moved at all except to slip away.

Perrin was quite clear in his own mind now that he hated Traill very much indeed, but he could not be very definitely sure of any reasons. There had been something once about an umbrella, and there was something else about Miss Desart, and there was even something about Garden Minimus; but none of these things were fixed very resolutely in his mind, and his thoughts slipped about like gold-fish in a pond.

It was quite certain, however, that Traill must not be allowed to go on like this, because he was a nuisance, and Perrin would sit for long hours whilst he was superintending examinations thinking about this and what he could do.

There were moments, even hours, when the consciousness of the two figures at his side and the weighty burden of his decision left him. He saw suddenly as clearly as he had ever seen, and he was frightened; it was like waking from an evil dream, and just when he was gazing back at it, frightened, even terrified, it would come slipping about him again, and the world would once more grow dark.

At last he was frightened at these intervals, because he seemed to realize then how dismal and unhappy it all was, and also how dangerous it was.

Once, during one of these clear moments, he was standing, a melancholy figure, by the iron gate, looking down the Brown Hill road, and Garden Minimus passed him. Perrin stopped him, and then when he saw the boy's round face and shining eyes, a little frightened now, and the mouth quivering a little, he had nothing to say.

At last he said, 'Oh!—Ah!—Garden—I haven't seen much of you lately. How do the exams go?'

Perrin had an absurd impulse to take the boy by the arm and ask him to be kind to him. He was so dreadfully unhappy.

But Garden was very frightened; he choked a little in his throat, and his eyes moved frantically down the white road as though appealing for help.

'Oh, very well, sir, thank you, sir—I—I couldn't do the geography this morning sir.'

There was a long pause. Garden gave frightened glances up and down the road.

'When do you go for—um, ah—your holidays, Garden?'

Garden looked up in Mr. Perrin's face, and suddenly, young though he was, felt that Mr.

Perrin was, as he put it afterwards, 'awfully sick about something—not ratty, you know, but jolly near blubbing.'

He had, with his friends, noticed that Perrin was 'jolly odd' during these days, but now this other struck him to the extinction of every other feeling. He had a sudden desire to help—after all, Old Pompous had been beastly decent to him—and then there came an overwhelming sensation of shyness, as though his feminine relations had suddenly appeared and claimed him in the company of his contemporaries. He looked down, rubbed one boot against the other, and then suddenly, with a murmured word about 'having to meet some fellows—beastly late,' was off.

Perrin watched him go and then turned slowly back towards the school buildings. The shadows were creeping about him again. He felt that the other Mr. Perrin was behind him. He walked stealthily, a little as a cat prowls. . . .

II

About this time he took great curiosity in Traill's bedroom. He had never been inside it—he knew only that plain brown door with marks near the bottom of it where the paint had been scratched.

But he sat now in his room and thought about it. He sat in a chair by the windows and looked across the room at his own door, at the square black lock and the shining brass handle. It was of course very easy to turn, and then he would be inside. It would be interesting to be inside—he would know then where the bed was, and the washing-stand, and the chairs . . . it might be useful to know.

He went to his own door and opened it, and looked very cautiously down the passage; there was no one there—it was all very silent. The sun of the December afternoon flooded the cold passage, and from downstairs the shouts of some boys floated up. . . . There were no other sounds.

He walked very softly down the passage, his head lowered, his hands behind his back. He stopped outside Traill's bedroom door and listened again—he was surprised to hear that his heart was beating very loudly indeed. He pushed the door open and looked inside. The bed was near the window—the sun flooded the room and shone on the silver-backed hair-brushes and the china basin and jug.

It was a very simple room, and the bed took up most of it: there was one photograph.

He went very softly up to it and saw that it was a photograph of Miss Desart—Miss Desart, smiling, out of doors with the sun on her dress.

He bent towards the photograph, over the china basin, and kissed it. Then he went out, closing the door softly behind him.

III

And the week wore away, and Monday came round. Thursday was Speech Day, and on Friday everybody went home; all marks and form lists had to be in the head master's room on Wednesday night before nine.

Perrin, on Monday evening, was vaguely conscious that he had corrected no papers at all. They lay about his room now in stacks—none of them were corrected. Some masters posted results as they corrected the papers; other masters left all the results until the end. It was not considered strange that Perrin had posted no results.

But he knew as he looked at these white sheets that he ought to have done something with them. He stood in the middle of the room with his hands to his head and wondered what he ought to have done. Why, of course, he ought to correct them—he ought to say what was good and what was bad.

He took up a large pile of them, and they almost slipped from his fingers because there were so many. He found that it was a paper on French Grammar. He looked at the slip with the questions.

'1. Give the preterite (singular only) and past participle of *donner, recevoir, laisser, s'asseoir* . . .'

Ah! *s'asseoir* was a hard one—he had always

found that that was difficult. He turned over the page:

'J'eu,
tu eus,
il eut'—

that looked wrong. . . .

Again, here was Simpson Minor—'Je fus, tu fus, il fut'—surely that was confused in some way.

The papers at the bottom slipped: he bent to prevent them falling, and all of them tipped over. They rose in a cloud about him, a white cloud, flying into the air, sailing to the other end of the room, diving under the table and into the fire-place, and a great white pile lay scattered wildly on the floor.

The silly papers stared at him:

'Je dors tous . . .'

'Il faut que . . .' 'I used to love my mother, but now I love my aunt . . .'

'Rule for the conjunctive and disjunctive pronouns . . .'

And then, Simpson Minor: 'Je fus, tu fus . . .'

He was infuriated with their silly, stupid faces. They lay there on the floor, staring up at him and making no attempt whatever to move. He was maddened by their impassivity. He began to stamp on them, and then to trample on them—he rushed about the room, uttering little cries and wildly stamping. . . .

And then something suddenly seemed to go in

his brain, and he stopped still. What was he doing? He bent feebly to pick them up, but he could not collect them. He sat down at his table with his head in his hands.

Then he gave up trying to correct them. After all, they were not the important thing—the important thing was between himself and Traill; that was what he must think about.

This was Monday, and on Friday every one would go away. He would go away, he supposed, with the rest: of course he would go to his mother. Traill would go away with Miss Desart . . . would he?

The other Mr. Perrin leant over and whispered in his ear.

It was from this moment that Mr. Perrin came to the definite decision that something must be done before Friday. He made five black marks with a pencil on the yellow wall-paper in his bedroom, and he would lie back on his bed at night, staring up at the marks whilst his candle guttered on the chair at his side. Monday, Tuesday, Wednesday, Thursday, Friday. . . . Monday passed, and he scratched another mark across the mark that he had already made. Tuesday passed, and that he also scratched out. Wednesday morning came.

Divinity was the only examination left except Repetition on Thursday morning: Wednesday afternoon was a half-holiday.

He gave out the Old Testament questions:

'1. Say what you know about the rebellion of Korah, Dathan, and Abiram: its cause and effects.

'2. Write briefly a life of Aaron . . .'

He found that now suddenly his brain was perfectly clear. To-day was Wednesday—before Friday he would kill Traill. The determination came to him perfectly plainly in the midst of these questions:

'6. Give context of: "Kill me, I pray thee, out of hand, if I have found favour in thy sight."

'"Let us make a captain and let us return into Egypt."

'"Is the Lord's hand waxed short?"'

He would kill Traill. He did not mind at all what happened to him afterwards. What did it matter? Perhaps he would kill himself. He was a complete failure; he had never been any use at all, and had only been there for people to laugh at and mock him.

If it had not been for Traill he might have been of use—he might have married Miss Desart. Traill had been against him in every way, and now the only thing that was left for him to do was to kill Traill. He hated Traill—of course he hated Traill; but it was not really because of that that he was going to kill Traill—it was only because he wanted to show all these people that he could do something: he was not useless, after all. They might laugh at him and call him Pompous, but, after all, the laugh would be on his side at the end. . . . Traill would not be able to kiss Miss Desart very much longer—another day, and he would never be able to kiss her again. . . . That was a pleasant thought.

Now that he had decided this question he felt a great deal happier and easier in his mind. There was no longer any self-pity. He had given God His opportunity—he had prayed to God and besought Him; he had tried very hard at the beginning of this term to go right and to be agreeable to people and to keep the other Mr. Perrin in the distance, but everything had been very hard, and that was God's fault for making it so hard.

He thought that he would surprise God by killing Traill. God would not be expecting that.

Still more would he surprise the place—Moffatt's—that place that had treated him so cruelly all these years. It would be a grand, big thing to kill his enemy.

On that Wednesday, half an hour before the midday dinner, he walked slowly, with his hands behind his bent back, through the long dining-hall. The long, black tables were laid for dinner, and beside every round, shining plate there lay two knives. These knives made a long glittering line right down the table, and the sun caught their gleaming steel and flashed from knife to knife. The sight of them fascinated Mr. Perrin—it was with a knife that he would kill Traill—he would cut Traill's throat. He picked them up, one after the other, and felt their edges—they were all wonderfully sharp. There were a great many of them—you could cut a great many throats with all those knives, but he did not want to cut any one else's throat except Traill's—Traill was his enemy.

At dinner that day he was pleasant and cheerful. He joked with the boys on either side of him and asked where they were going for the holidays.

'Ah! Cromer—um—yes, very pleasant. Our little friend will amuse himself hugely at Cromer, no doubt. Sure to over-eat on Christmas Day. Um, yes—and you, Larkin, where do you go? . . . Ah! Whitby—long way. Yes, able to read your holiday task in the train.'

He sent the servant out to sharpen the carving-knife, and when it was brought back he attacked the mutton in the most furious way, scattering the gravy over the cloth.

After dinner he stood above the playing-fields watching the clouds sail across the sky. It was a very grey-coloured day, but there was the light of the sun behind it, so that everything shone without colour but with a transparency as though one should be able to see other lights and colours behind it.

Perrin thought that he had never seen the clouds assume such curious shapes—perhaps they were not clouds at all, but rather creatures of the sky that only his eye could see, just as it was only his eye that could see the other Mr. Perrin. There were birds with long, bending necks, and fat, round-faced animals with only one eye, and stiff, angular creatures with wings and legs like sticks, and then again there were splendid galleons with sails unfurled, and cathedral towers and trees and mountain ranges—they were all very strange and beautiful, and perhaps this was the last time that he would see them.

Then he saw, passing down the path to the right and walking fast in the direction of the road, two figures; another glance, and he saw that they were Miss Desart and Traill—there was no doubt at all that that was Miss Desart in her grey dress, and that man with his swinging stick was Traill.

The sight of them together suddenly roused him to fury; it would be amusing to kill Traill now, there, before Miss Desart. He did not know how he would do it, perhaps he would spring on to Traill's back from behind and strangle him with his hands.

And so, with the other Mr. Perrin at his ear, he followed them down the path.

It was a day of ghosts—even the brown colour of the earth of the hill that so seldom left it was gone to-day. It was not a cold day, and one felt that the sun was burning with intense heat in some neighbouring place, but grey wisps of mist crept in and out of the black, naked hedges, and, at the bottom of the hill, banks of mist lay, hiding the cottages of the village.

The two figures passed in front of him down the hill and became, like the rest of the day, grey and misty, and he followed them, stealthily, with his hands behind his back. Their heads were very close together, and he could see that they were talking very eagerly. They were discussing, probably, their plans for the holidays, and it pleased him to think that he would make all their plans of no avail. It pleased the other Mr. Perrin also.

They passed down the village street and then up the steep narrow path to the road that led along the top of the cliffs. At the top of the path the mists had cleared again, and the rocks, hidden at the floor of the sea by grey vapour, stood as it were in mid-air, their black edges piercing the sky. When Mr. Perrin climbed to the top of the path, the other figures had preceded him some way along it and were almost hidden by boulders. He hastened a little so that he might keep them in sight, and then he hung back a little lest he should be too close to them. They were still talking very eagerly and crossed down a strong path that led to a sheltered cove. At the bottom of this they sat down on the sand, and Perrin hid behind a rock and watched them.

The world was terribly still, because, although there was a wind that made the clouds race along, it seemed to leave the sea alone, and the water made the very faintest sound as it touched the beach and faded away into the mist again.

Mr. Perrin found that his legs were very tired, and so he sat down behind his stone and peered out at them. They sat very close together on the sand, and then Traill put out his arm and Miss Desart crept into it and sat there with her head against his shoulder. And when Perrin saw that, he knew that he never could do anything to Traill whilst Miss Desart was there. A dreadful feeling of home-sickness came over him, and his eyes filled with tears. It was so unfair, so unfair. If only there had been someone there to whom he could have done that: if only there had ever been any one in his life! . . . but he dashed the tears from his eyes. He had not come there to cry—he had come there for vengeance, and then, at that thought, he wondered whether after all he were not so poor a creature that he would never be able to kill any one. Supposing he were to miss even this chance of achievement! There, behind his rock, he tried to gather together all his reasons for hating Traill; but he couldn't think properly, and the pebbles on which he was sitting were pressing into his trousers, and his neck was hurting because he craned it so. At any rate he was very uncomfortable, and as he could certainly do nothing whilst Miss Desart was there, he had better go away. And so he got up very slowly and painfully from behind his rock and went timidly up the path again.

IV

And that night, after going the round of the dormitories for the last time, he went into his room and closed his door with the clear determination of settling things up.

His head had not been so clear for weeks. He saw at once that he had corrected no papers and that something must be done about that.

He sat down, and with the term's marks beside him, made out imaginary examination lists. Of course it was all very wrong, but it was for the last time, and he had, after all, put the boys in the order in which they would probably occur. This took him about an hour.

Then he took all the files of examination papers and tore them up. This took a long time, and they filled, at last, his waste-paper basket to overflowing. Then he sat down to write to his mother.

'DEAR OLD LADY,—This is the last time that you will see or hear from me. Do not regret it or anything that I have done, because I am no good, and am just a failure. There is £100 in the bank which I have saved, and you will get things with it. Sell my things; they will bring a little. I love you very much, old lady, but I am no good.—Your loving son,

'VINCENT PERRIN.'

He fastened up the letter and addressed it to:

Mrs. Perrin,
Holly Cottage,
Bubblewick,
Bucks.

Just as he finished it he heard eleven o'clock strike. He waited until the clocks had ended, then he opened his door and looked down the passage. It was quite silent. He walked quietly down the stairs, down the lower passage, and so to the dining-room.

Here the long tables were laid for breakfast. He paused at one of the tables and chose one of the knives; they did not seem very sharp, and he tried others on the back of his hand. At last he had selected one and put it under his coat. He returned to his room and closed his door. When he got there he stood in the middle of his room, and looked stupidly at the knife. What had he got it for? There was Traill next door . . . of course.

But he could not do anything now. He had fancied that when one had got the knife, then the next thing was to go straight and do something with it. But he found that he could not, that he could not move from where he was, and that his hand was shaking as though with an ague.

The knife dropped on to the floor with a sharp sound, and he sank into a chair. What a wretched, miserable creature he was, after all! There was nothing fine about him—there was nothing fine about any one at Moffatt's—they were all a miserable lot . . . and to-morrow there would be speeches and prizes and cheering! What a funny thing life was!

But it was no use thinking about life with that knife on the floor. It was quite clear that he wasn't going to do anything to-night—he might just as well go to bed. His headache was dreadfully bad, and he was shivering all over. He put the knife into a drawer and blew out his lamp.

He hated the dark—he had always hated it—and so he hurried into his bedroom and tried to light his candle, but his hand was shaking so that it was a long time before he could strike a match, and he cursed the matches feebly and felt inclined to cry.

He was a long time undressing and sat on the edge of the bed in his shirt and looked at his long thin legs and hated them; then he saw the black marks on the yellow paper, and he scratched another off. . . . At last he blew out the candle and got into bed.

He seemed to fall asleep all at once and was aware that he was asleep—but after a time he felt that, although he was asleep, he was conscious of someone watching him. He opened his eyes and saw that the other Mr. Perrin was sitting by his bed, watching him, and although the room was quite dark, the grey figure was in some way luminous, so that he could see that he wore a long, grey cloak and that his features were exactly the same as his own. He was forced against his will to get out of bed and to follow the other Mr. Perrin out of the house, down the long, white road, down to the sea. Here they were in that little cove where Traill and Miss Desart had been that afternoon. They sat with their backs against the rocks, and in all the air there was a strange, uncertain light, and the sea came over the shore in sullen, dreamy movements, as a tired woman's fingers move when she is sewing.

Then Mr. Perrin saw that down the beach there passed a long procession of grey, bending figures with heavy burdens on their backs. Their faces were white and hopeless, and their hands, with long, white fingers, hung at their sides.

He was conscious of some great feeling of injustice—that this must not be allowed—and an overmastering impulse to call out that it was all wrong and to run forward and relieve them of their burdens—but he could not move nor utter any sound. Then suddenly he recognized faces that he knew, and he saw White and Birkland and Comber and Dormer and then—his own.

He gave a great cry and broke from his companion and rushed swiftly back up the white road, in through the black gates, up the stairs, and into his room.

He stood in the middle of his room and felt suddenly cold. To his surprise he saw that the moon was shining through the window, although there had been no moon on the beach. The room was so bright that he could distinguish every object perfectly—and then he realized slowly that things were different. Those silver-backed hair-brushes were not his, his bed was not there—that photograph . . .

Someone was in the bed.

For an instant his heart stopped beating. There was a draught between the window and the door . . . someone else was in the bed; he had been walking in his sleep; he was in Traill's room.

He could see Traill quite clearly now, lying with one hand on the counterpane, his head on an arm. He was fast asleep, and his mouth was smiling.

Mr. Perrin shook from head to foot. Here was his opportunity—here was his enemy fast asleep . . . now. He stepped nearer to the bed—he bent over the face. Traill's pyjama-jacket was open at the neck . . . it would be very easy.

Then suddenly, with a little cry and his face in his hands, he crept from the room.

CHAPTER XIII

MR. PERRIN LISTENS WHILST THEY ALL MAKE SPEECHES

I

THE next day, its brilliant sun and hard, shining cold, brought in its train great things.

The last day of the Christmas term was in some ways greater than the last day of the summer term, because it was a more private family affair.

One addressed one's ancestors, one arrayed one's traditions, one fashioned one's history, with flags and flowers and orations, but it was in the midst of the family that it was done.

Parents—mothers and fathers and cousins—were indeed there, but they, too, must recognize that it was not for their immediate individual Johnny or Charles that these things were done, but rather for the great worship and recognition of Sir Marmaduke Boniface.

Sir Marmaduke Boniface has hitherto received no mention in this slender history, but his importance in any chronicle of Moffatt's cannot be over-estimated. He was a Cornish magnate, living and dying some hundred years ago, growing rich in the pursuit of jam, building large stone mansions out of that same delicacy, fat, pompous, and fading at last into a heavy stone monument in the corner of the church at the bottom of the Brown Hill—a great man in his day and in his place, amongst other things the founder of Moffatt's.

It was not very long ago; outside the confines of Cornwall he had been perhaps but vaguely recognized—perchance, perchance, the surest foundation of an extravagant record. . . . No matter, here we have our tradition, and let us make the best possible use of it.

But this Marmadukery—a hideous word, but it serves—spread far beyond that stout originator. It was the spirit of the public school, the *esprit de corps* signified by the School song (it began 'Procul in Cornubia,' and was violently shouted at stated intervals during the year), the splendid appeal 'to our fathers who have played in these fields before us'—this was the cry that these banners and orations signified. Moffatt's was not a very old school, true—but shout enough about some founder or other and the smallest boy will have tears in his eyes and a proud swelling at his breast. Sir Marmaduke becomes medieval, mystic, 'the great, good man' of history, and Moffatt's is 'one of our good old schools. There 's nothing like our public school system, you know—has its faults, of course; but tradition—that 's the thing.'

The stout figure of Sir Marmaduke hangs heavy

over the day. Every one feels it—every one feels a great many other things as well, but Sir Marmaduke is the Thing.

He was the Thing in some vague, blind way even to Mrs. Comber, so that he kept coming into the confused but happy conversation to which she treated anxious parents on the morning of this great day. Mothers arrived in great numbers on these occasions, and these three great days of the three terms were to Mrs. Comber the happiest and most confused events in the year. They marked an approaching freedom, they marked the immediate return of her own children, and they marked an amazing number of things that ought to be done at once, with the confusing feeling about Sir Marmaduke also in the air.

But to-day she was happy; this horrible, terrible term was almost over. She had been so sure that something dreadful was going to happen, and nothing dreadful had happened, after all. They were safe—or almost safe—and her dear Isabel and Isabel's young man would be out of the place before they knew where they were. Then her own Freddie had last night, suddenly, before going to bed, taken her in his arms and kissed her as he had never kissed her before. Oh! things were going to be all right . . . they were escaping for a time at any rate. In the thought of the holidays, of a month's freedom, everything that had happened during the term was swiftly becoming faint and vague and distant.

Now she was smiling in her sitting-room with four mothers about her, one very fat and one very thin, one in blue and one in grey, and they all sat very stiff in their chairs and listened to what she had to say.

She had a great deal to say, because she was feeling so happy, and happiness always provoked volubility, but she made the mistake of talking to all four of them at once, and they, in vain, like anglers at a pool, flung, desperately, hurried little sentences at her, but secured no attention. Beyond and above it all was the shadow of Sir Marmaduke.

But her happiness, when she drove them at length from her, caught at the advancing figure of Isabel, with a cry and a clasp of the hand: 'My dear!—no, we 've only got a minute because lunch is early—one o'clock, and cold—you don't mind, do you, dear; but there 's to be *such* a dinner to-night, and I 've just had four mothers, and wise isn't the word for what I 've been, although I confused all their children as I always do, bless their little hearts! But, oh! the term 's over, and I could go on my knees and thank Heaven that it is, because I 've never hated anything so much, and if it had lasted another week I should have struck off Mrs. Dormer's head for the way she 's been treating you, for dead sure certain——'

'Archie 's not coming back, you know,' Isabel interrupted.

'Oh, my dear, I knew. He went and saw Moy-Thompson last week, and of course it 's the wisest thing, and I only wish my Freddie was as young and we 'd be off from here to-morrow.' She stopped and sighed a little and looked through the window at the hard, shining ground, the stiff, bare trees, the sharp outline of the buildings. 'But it 's no use wishing,' she went on cheerfully enough, 'and we won't any of us think of next term at all, but only of the blessed month of freedom that 's in front of us.' Her voice softened; she put her hand on Isabel's arm. 'All the same, my dear, I 'm glad you and Archie are getting away from it all. It was touching him, you know.'

'Yes, I saw it,' the girl answered. 'And I don't want him to schoolmaster again if he can help it. I think with father's help he 'll be able to get a government office of some sort.' She hesitated, then said, smiling a little, 'Are you and Mr. Comber——' She stopped.

'Yes, my dear,' said Mrs. Comber huskily, 'we are—and there 's no doubt that things are better than they have been. I suppose marriage is always like that; there 's the thrilling time at first, and then you find it isn't there any longer and you 've got to make up your mind to getting along. Things rub you up, you know, and I 'm sure I 've been as tiresome as anything, and then there 's a good big row and the air 's cleared—and shall I wear that big yellow hat or the black one this afternoon?'

'The black one fits the day better,' said Isabel absent-mindedly. She was wondering whether the time would ever come when she and Archie would feel ordinary about each other.

'But isn't it funny,' she went on, 'that here we are at the end of the term, and already, with the holidays beginning, all our quarrels and fights about things like that silly umbrella are seeming impossible? It was all too absurd, and yet I was as angry as any one.'

'It all comes,' said Mrs. Comber, 'of our living too close. Now that we 're going to spread out over the holidays, we 're as friendly as anything, although really, my dear, I hate Mrs. Dormer as much as ever'—which was difficult to believe when that lady arrived at a quarter-past two to pick up Mrs. Comber and Isabel and to go with them to the prize-giving.

Her dress was obviously very stiff and difficult, with a high, black neck to it, with little ridges of whalebone all round it, and out of this she spoke and smiled. The two ladies were very pleasant to one another as they walked down the path to the school hall.

'And where are you going for your Christmas vacation, Mrs. Comber?'

'I really don't know. It depends so much on the boys and the housemaid. I mean the house-maid 's given notice, you know, because I had to speak to her about breathing when handing round the vegetables; and she gave notice on the spot, as they all do when I speak to them, and unless I can get another, I really don't think I shall ever be able to get away.'

'Really, what servants are coming to!' Mrs. Dormer was struggling with her collar like a dog. 'Poor Mrs. Comber, I *am* so sorry—of course management 's the thing, but we haven't all the gift and can't expect to have it.'

'And, Mrs. Dormer, I do hope that you are going to be here over Christmas, so that we can keep each other company. It would be so nice if you and Mr. Dormer would come to us on Boxing evening, even if I haven't got a housemaid; and I heard of a very likely one from Mrs. Rose yesterday—quite a nice girl she sounded—who 's been under-parlourmaid at Colonel Forster's now for the last five years, and never a fault to find with her except a tendency to catching cold, which made her sniff at times.'

'Oh, thank you, dear Mrs. Comber; but my husband and I are hoping to spend a few days in London about that time. Otherwise we should have loved——'

For so much charity is the presence of Sir Marmaduke Boniface responsible.

II

Sir Marmaduke, and all that his coming signified, was also responsible for clearing the air in other directions. Young Traill found, on this morning, that people were very much pleasanter to him than they had hitherto been. The coming holidays were obviously to be a truce, and, as he was not returning next term, it was an end of things so far as he was concerned. He could not feel proud of it all. The events of the term had shown him that he was not nearly so fine a fellow as he had thought himself. His pride, his temper, his irritation—all these things were lions with which he had never fought before: now they must always, for the future, be consciously kept in check.

He was tired, exhausted, worn out. He was very glad that he was going away—now he would be able to have Isabel to himself, and they might, together, forget this horrible nightmare of a term. He looked on the buildings of Moffatt's as the iron prison of some hideous dream. He could not sleep for the thought of it. Last night he had had some bad dream . . . he could not remember now what it had been, but he had wakened suddenly, in a great panic, to imagine that someone was closing his door. Of course it had only been the wind, but he hoped that he would sleep properly to-night.

At any rate he was glad that people were going to be pleasant to him on this last day of the term. The stout Miss Madder, Dormer, Clinton—they all seemed to be sorry that he was going, in spite of all the trouble that he had made. He did not think of Perrin. . . .

Then he suddenly remembered Birkland. He would go and say good-bye to him.

He climbed the steep stairs and found the little man busily packing. The floor was covered with packing-cases, books lay about in piles, and the air was full of dust.

'Hallo!' said Traill, coughing, in the doorway, 'what 's all this?'

'Hallo!' said Birkland, looking up. 'I 'm glad you 've come. I was coming round to see you, if you hadn't. I 'm off for good.'

'Off for good!' Traill stared in astonishment.

'Well, for good or bad. The things that have happened this term have finally screwed me up to a last attempt. One more struggle before I die—nothing can be worse than this—I gave notice last week.'

'What are you going to do?' asked Traill.

'I don't know—it 's mad enough, I expect. But I 've saved a tiny bit of money that will keep me for a time. I shall have a shot at anything. Nothing can be as bad as this—nothing!'

He stood up, looking grim and scant enough in his shirt sleeves with dust on his cheeks and his hair on end.

'Well, I 'm damned!' said Traill. 'Well, after all, I 'm on the same game. I don't know what I 'm going to do, either. We 're both in the same box.'

'Oh,' said Birkland, 'you 've got youth and a beautiful lady to help you. I 'm alone, and most of the spirit 's knocked out of me after twenty years of this; but I 'm going to have a shot—so wish me luck!'

'Why, of course I do,' said Traill, coming up to him. 'We 'll do it together—we 'll see heaps of each other.'

'Ah, heaps!' said Birkland, shaking his head. 'No, I 'm too dry and dusty a stick by this time for young fellows like you. No, I 'm better alone. But I 'll come and see you one day.'

'You were quite right,' said Traill suddenly, 'in what you said about the place the evening at the beginning of the term when I came in to see you. You were quite right.'

'Poor boy,' said Birkland, looking at him affectionately, 'you had a hard dose of it. Perhaps it was all for the best, really. It drove you out. If I 'd been treated to that kind of row at the beginning, I mightn't have been here twenty years. And, after all, you met Miss Desart here.'

'Yes,' said Traill, 'that makes it worth it fifty times over.'

'And now,' went on Birkland grimly, 'this afternoon you shall see the closing scene of our pageant. You shall see our glory, our tradition. You will hear the head of our body state his satisfaction with the term's work, proclaim his delight at the friendly spirit that pervades the school, allude, through the great Sir Marmaduke Boniface, maker of strawberry jam, to our ancient and honourable tradition in which we all, from the eldest to the youngest, have our humble share.' He spread his arms. 'Oh, the mockery of it! To get out of it!—to get out of it! And now at last, after twenty years, I 'm going. If it hadn't been for you, Traill, I believe I 'd be here still. Well, perhaps it 's to breaking stones on a road that I 'm going . . . at any rate, it won't be this.'

And so, here too, Sir Marmaduke Boniface is remembered and has his influence.

III

But with all these fine spirits, with all this stir and friendly feeling, with all this preparation for a great event, Mr. Perrin had little to do. This morning had, in no way, been for him a reconciling or a triumph at approaching freedom. After some three or four hours' troubled and confused sleep he awoke to the humiliating, maddening consciousness that he had again, now for a second time, missed his chance.

This one thing that he had thought he could do he had missed once more; not even at this last, blind vengeance was he any good.

To-morrow it would be too late; Traill, his enemy, would be gone, they would all be gone, and he would return, next term, the same insignificant creature at whom they had all laughed for so long; and then it would be worse than ever, because Traill would have escaped him, and in the distant ages it would be told how once there had been a young man, straight from the university, who had flung him to the ground and trampled on him, and beaten him, in all probability with his own umbrella. . . .

Ah, no! it was not to be borne—the thing must be done; there must be no missing of an opportunity this third time.

He heard the Repetition that morning with a vacant mind. Pomfret-Walpole knew nothing about it, but for once in his life he suffered no punishment. Perrin thought afterwards that Garden Minimus had looked at him as though he would like to speak to him, but he could not think of Garden Minimus now—there were other more important things to think about.

Of course it must be done that night—there was only one night left. Afterwards he thought that he would go down to the sea and drown himself. He had heard that drowning was rather pleasant.

His mind was busy, all that morning, with the things that every one would say afterwards. He wished very much that he could stay behind in some way that he might hear what they said. At any rate, they would be able to laugh at him no longer; he would appear to all of them as something terrible, portentous, awful . . . that, at any rate, was a satisfaction. Miss Desart, of course, would be sorry. That was a pity, because he did not wish to hurt Miss Desart; but, in the end, it would be all for the best, because she was much too good for a man like Traill, and would only be unhappy if she married him.

What a scene there would be when they found Traill in bed with his throat cut!—no, they would not laugh at him again!

He spoke to nobody that morning; but, when Repetition was over, he went back to his room and sat there, quite still, in his chair, looking in front of him, with the door closed.

And then Traill came up and spoke to him just as he was on his way up to the school for the speeches.

He smiled and said, 'Oh, I say, Perrin, do let us make it all up—now that term is over, and I 'm not coming back. I do hate to think that we should not part friends—it 's all been my stupid fault, and I am so very sorry.'

But Perrin did not stop nor answer. He walked straight up the path with his eyes looking neither to the left nor the right. After all, you couldn't shake hands with a man whose throat you were going to cut in the evening. He heard Traill's exasperated 'Oh, very well,' and then he passed into Big School. He stepped into the hall as unobtrusively as possible. The boys were always there first, and it was their way to cheer the masters as they came in. If you were very popular, they cheered you loudly; if you were unpopular, they cheered you not at all. Perrin had no illusions about his popularity, and the silence on his entrance did not therefore surprise him, but matters were not improved by the roar of cheering that greeted Traill. Ah, well! they would never cheer him again.

The boys were placed in rows down the room according to their forms, and the masters sat where they pleased. Perrin stationed himself in a corner by the wall at the back; he fastened his eyes on the platform and kept them there until the end of the ceremonies—no one noticed him—no one spoke to him—not for him were their songs and festivals.

The raised platform at the end of the hall was surrounded with flowers, and ranged against the wall, seated on hard, uncertain chairs, were the Governing Body, or as many of the Governing Body as had spared time to come.

These were for the most part large, serious, elderly gentlemen, with stout bodies, and shining, beady eyes; their immovability implied that they considered that the business would be sooner over were they passive and as non-existent as possible—they all wore a considerable amount of watch-chain.

In front of them was a long black table, and on this were ranged the prizes—a number of impossibly shiny volumes that might have been biscuit-tins, for all the reading that they seemed to contain. Beside them in a wooden arm-chair was seated a little man like a sparrow, in patent-leather boots and a high, white collar, whose smile was intermittent, but regular.

This was Sir Arthur Spalding, who had been asked to give away the prizes, because ten other gentlemen had been invited and refused. On the other side of the table the Rev. Moy-Thompson tried to express geniality and authority by the curve of his fingers and the bend of his head; he stroked his beard at intervals. In the front row the ladies were seated: Mrs. Comber, large and smiling, in purple; Mrs. Moy-Thompson, endeavouring to escape her husband's eye, but drawn thither continually as though by a magnet; the Misses Madder, Mrs. Dormer, Isabel, and many parents.

The proceedings opened with a speech from the Rev. Moy-Thompson. He alluded, of course, in the first place to Sir Marmaduke Boniface, 'our founder, hero, and example'; then by delicate stages to Sir Arthur Spalding, whose patent-leather boots simply shone with delight at the pleasant things that were said. This preface over, he dilated on the successes of the term. K. Somers had been made a Commissioner of Police in Orang-Mazu-Za (cheers); W. Binnors had been fifteenth in an examination that had something to do with Tropical Diseases (more cheers); M. Watson had received the College Essay Prize at St. Catherine's College, Cambridge; and C. Duffield had obtained a second class in the first part of the Previous Examination at the same university (frantic cheering, because Duffield had been last year's captain of the Rugby football). All this, Mr. Moy-Thompson said, was exceedingly encouraging, and they could not help reflecting that Sir Marmaduke Boniface, were he conscious of these successes, would be extremely pleased (cheers). Passing on to the present term he was delighted to be able to say that never, in all his long period as head master, could he remember a more equable and energetic term (cheers). As a term it had been marked perhaps by no events of special magnitude, but rather by the cordial friendliness of all those concerned. Masters and boys, they had all worked together with a will. It was a familiar saying that 'a nation was blessed that had no history'—well, that applied to such a term as the one just concluded (cheers). If he might allude once more to their excellent Founder, he was quite sure that Sir Marmaduke Boniface was precisely the kind of man to rejoice in this spirit of friendship (cheers). He must here allude for a moment to his staff. Surely a head master had never been surrounded with so pleasant a body of men—men who understood exactly the kind of *esprit de corps* necessary if a school's work were to be properly carried on; men who put aside all private feelings for the one great purpose of making Moffatt's a great school—that was, he truly believed, the one aim and object of every man and boy in Moffatt's—they might be sure that was the one and only aim and object that he ever kept before him. He had nothing more to do but introduce Sir Arthur Spalding, who would give away the prizes.

Mr. Moy-Thompson sat down, hot and inspired, amidst a burst of frantic cheering and clapping, but was suddenly chilled by the consciousness of Mr. Perrin's eyes glaring at him in the strangest manner across the room. He shifted his chair a little to the left, so that a boy's head intervened. The Governing Body at the conclusion of his speech moved their heads to the right, then to the left, smiled once, and resumed their immovability.

Sir Arthur Spalding was nervous, but found courage to say that he believed in our public schools—that was the thing that made men of us—he should never forget what he himself owed to Harrow. He should like to say one thing to the boys—that they were not to think that winning prizes was everything. We couldn't all win prizes; let those who failed to obtain them remember that 'slow and steady wins the race.' It wasn't always the boys who won prizes who got on best afterwards. No—um—ah—he never used to win prizes at school himself. It wasn't always the boys—here he pulled himself up and remembered that he had said it before. There was something else that he'd wanted to say, but he'd quite forgotten what it was. Here he was conscious of Mr. Perrin's eyes, and thought that he'd never seen anything so discouraging. He did not seem to be able to escape them. What a dangerous-looking man!

So he hurriedly concluded. Just one word he'd like to leave them from our great poet Tennyson——! He looked for the little piece of paper on which he had written the verse. He could not find it; he searched his pockets—no—where had he put it? Lady Spalding, in the third row, suffered horrible agonies. He recovered himself and was vague. He would advise them all to read Tennyson, a fine poet, a very fine poet—yes—and now he would give away the prizes.

He drew a deep breath and moved to the back of the table; he could see that horrible man's eyes no longer, enough to drive any man's ideas out of his head.

They began with a minute boy who had won the First Form Prize. He was very small and very hot, and his boots made a noise like a tree blown by the wind. Sir Arthur talked to him a little, asked him what he was going to be when he grew up, and was preparing to be pleasant when he found to his horror that the next two boys to receive prizes were waiting at his elbow and breathing heavily and anxiously in his ear. After that he made no more speeches, but hurried along.

This giving of prizes was a dreary affair, and any excitement or emotion that there may have been over the earlier stages soon evaporated entirely.

There was a feeling of restlessness throughout the hall, and the signal for the School song was received with relief by every one. The boys stood up on the benches, and presently 'Procul in Cornubia' rang through the building. The noise was terrific, and every one except the boys was glad when that also was over.

'God save the King!' followed and Sir Marmaduke's shadow was appeased.

All this had taken some time, and it was quite dark when they all came out into the air again and hurried to have tea.

IV

Mr. Perrin went back to his room. He lit his lamp and sat down in his arm-chair. Now that the prize-giving was over, it seemed to have cleared the air. There was nothing now between himself and Traill. He had done with the school, he had done with schoolmastering. He was at last alone with his enemy.

What a long business it had been! That first meeting on the first day of term—he had liked him then—then his impertinence, his conceit, his lack of deference. Then things like the bath and the paper—little things—then the quarrel in that very room—then—the umbrella! —good heavens, how long ago that seemed! Then Miss Desart . . . yes, from the first he had been his enemy. He had taken everything from him, even Garden Minimus. He supposed that people would say that he had been his own enemy, that it had been all his own fault. Well, that was not true altogether, because he had meant to do well this term, he had meant to try. But everything had gone wrong. He had failed at everything . . . always. And his headaches. Yes, life had treated him very cruelly, and now, at the end of everything, he was going to get back on it. He had always prayed to God to give him his chance, and God had never given it to him—so now he must take it himself. God would be sorry that so fine a young fellow as Traill should be killed; He would much rather that he, Perrin, should die.

Well, for once, God should be outwitted. It was his revenge.

He took the knife out of the drawer and looked at it. He laid it on the table beside him.

The hours passed. The bell for supper rang. There was to be a concert at the Upper School. Soon he could hear them going to it, with laughter and shouting—Traill was taking them up, probably. . . . Well, it was the last concert that he would ever hear.

There was absolute stillness in the place. No sound at all. The lamp had not enough oil, and at last it flickered and went out. The room was in absolute darkness, but Mr. Perrin thought that he would not go to bed, because then he might go to sleep.

So he sat there, staring into the dark, with the knife on the table beside him.

CHAPTER XIV

MR. PERRIN MAKES GOOD

I

NEVERTHELESS, Mr. Perrin slept.

His head fell forward on his lap, and with his hands clenched tightly; the hours crept darkly about him, and the first grey dawn came, and still he did not waken. The knife lay, through all these hours, gleaming on the table; but he did not dream about it, or about anything: his was a sleep of sheer exhaustion with all the turmoil and distress that his poor head had suffered during these last weeks hanging down upon him like a heavy weight.

Could his face have been seen during those dark morning hours, he would have looked neither pompous nor avenging, but only pathetic, with his ragged wild moustache, and the heavy grey lines beneath his eyes, and his white, drawn cheeks—someone for whom life had been too much, someone who should, in spite of himself. have been treated kindly, with tenderness, someone who had once had possibilities. . . .

II

When the distant clocks struck eight he awoke with a start and realized at once what had happened. He jumped to his feet and counted the remaining strokes with a passionate sensation of protest. He had nearly missed his chance again! He could go and sleep when the deed to which he had, so firmly and resolutely, strung himself was waiting to be done!

He looked at the table and saw the knife. The sun would soon be up, and then everything would be light, and what he had to do must be done in the dark. He looked at the knife, and his knees trembled beneath him. What he had to do must be done in the dark. . . . And then he knew that he was faced at last with the inevitable last moment. There was to be no further choice after this. If he did not do it now, within the next half-hour, it could never be done at all! He picked up the knife, and it fell clattering from his hand. He picked it up from the floor and looked at it.

Well, it *must* be done—he set his teeth. His hated enemy should laugh at him no more, the world should laugh at him no more; he should be an emblem of terror, of horror—a portentous vengeance—he, Perrin, at whom they had once mocked. And so, quivering and shaking, the knife in his hand, he went to the door. The room was very dark, and he stumbled against the furniture and bruised his leg against the chair. He cursed and blinked his eyes and then yawned, because he was still very sleepy.

His hand trembled on the latch—then he turned it and looked round down the passage. It was all terribly silent and quite dark, except for a faint grey light that hung, like a mist, about the corners and along the ground. It hung about Traill's door, and the dark outline of it could be very distinctly seen.

The sweat poured down Mr. Perrin's face; he had set his teeth grimly, but the silence of it all was so appalling.

If only he could have worked himself into a rage, if only those moments when he would willingly have killed Traill could return!—but now here, in this cold passage, it was all so absurd, so deliberate, so frightening.

And yet, on the other hand, if the night passed and nothing had been done, things were worse than ever—Perrin was beaten.

He moved very stealthily and cautiously, with his hand against the wall-paper, a step along the passage. Then there was a sudden sound, coming on the silence like a stone flung into a pool; Mr. Perrin nearly screamed—his heart was a hammer beating against his chest, and he stumbled rather than stepped back into his door.

Then, with staring eyes, with a hot, burning

mouth, with a hand that gripped the knife until it hurt, he beheld a miracle—Traill's door opened. It was opened and quickly shut—someone stepped quietly out; it was Traill himself.

The place swam about Mr. Perrin, and he wondered whether he were, as he had been last week, caught with a ghostly Traill who followed him about wherever he went. But that other Traill had always slipped away when he looked at it—this Traill was there with a solidity about which there could be no possible question; there with a Norfolk jacket turned up about his ears, a grey cap, grey trousers, and at once swiftly turning down the passage and disappearing.

So Perrin, staring with frantic eyes, saw that the gods gave him his chance in no uncertain measure. He had asked for it; now he must take it. Here was his victim before him, ready to his hand—there must be no hanging back. He slipped the knife into his coat, and crept down the passage very softly, lest Traill should hear; moreover, it was after eight, and already the school servants must be about. He did not know where Traill was going—he must keep him in sight. The grey figure passed round the curve at the bottom of the stairs, down the long passage, and round the curve of the next staircase: Mr. Perrin followed very silently. His heart was still beating tumultuously, and he now had a frantic desire that Traill should not stop—he did not know what he would do if Traill stopped. Once he felt that he could not go on, and he leant against the wall to get his breath—then he stumbled on once more.

Traill crossed the lower passage, through the dining-hall, with its shining cloths and plates, into the outer hall; there he turned the locks of the hall door, and, closing it gently behind him, but without locking it, passed outside. Perrin followed.

As the coolness and dark mystery of the garden met him, he drew a great breath. Although it was so dark, the trees in the hedges hung in the air, a deeper black, like great animals waiting about the wall of the buildings. There was that stir in the air that always foreruns the rising sun, so that the world seemed peopled with life that was, as it were, holding its breath before the signal to break into sound. Mr. Perrin could hear, even as he waited that instant by the door, that there were innumerable things stirring in the warm, wet earth at his feet—this sense of the imminence of some preconcerted signal gave Perrin an added urgency. If all things round him were going to happen so immediately, if the world were suddenly in another five minutes to burst into light, and all these animals and things that grew in the ground were to be witnesses of his action, then all the more must that action be swift. He saw that Traill had hesitated a moment by the big iron gates—they were only a few yards away, and his grey figure was outlined in the dark—but soon the gates were opened, and Traill stood in the road. Perrin, hanging by the dark wall of the hedge, followed him. He had no cap on his head and only slippers on his feet, and he thought that it was very cold; his teeth were chattering so loudly that he was afraid lest Traill should hear.

Traill was walking down the hill now very slowly, his hands in his pockets and his head in the air, as though he were taking the freshness of it in, and Perrin followed him like a shadow, sometimes running a step or two, and then stopping for a moment, and crouching as though he thought that Traill would turn round, and Perrin's one thought was that he would catch a terrible cold, and in any case he might suddenly sneeze—and then Traill would see him, and then——!

As he crept thus miserably down the road, he watched with anxiety the gathering brightness in the sky—the way the lighter grey came in sheets and layers over the darker grey; and the sound of a little wind, rising from the heart of the road, seemed to announce in some mysterious fashion the rising sun. The wind whispered about the hedges, the stones of the road began to shine whitely from their dark surface, the trees were more sharply defined in their arrows and hoops of black—the little church clock struck quarter-past eight.

Traill paused near the bottom of the wood and finally turned through a wicket-gate, over a path through the fields that led to the cliff road.

Mr. Perrin followed him: his slippers hung loosely about him, his socks were wet, his moustache and hair draggled with damp; but his fingers were twitching and his breath came sharply, as though he had been running. The dark grass rose about his feet, and the bending hill above him leant, with its dark shoulder, upon him, with its rounded shape cutting into the grey sky. Traill passed in front, shadowed in outline; at a turn of the fields there came suddenly upon them both the full plunge of the sea. Now they were on the cliff road, and Perrin knew that at its edge were the black rocks and the sands below; here the cliff was not high, and the fall was not far, but further along the road the depth was tremendous. . . .

The sea was as space, and the indefinite grey of the sky—only the sand of the beach was a little whiter than the grey of the sea—and far out through the mist the first stirring of the cloud, with flecks and bars of silver light, showed the advancing sun. Suddenly Traill stopped and faced the sea. He took a pipe out of his pocket and felt for matches. Perrin was quite close to him. He found to his increasing horror that he could not stop. He was stumbling along, his head hanging, his shoes clapping behind him on the pebbly path. He seemed to have no control over his legs, because they were trembling so, and between his clenched teeth there came forth little exclamations like 'Oh!' and 'Ah!' and 'My!'—

gasps. Suddenly his loose slipper caught in a pebble, and down he came, catching at the air and uttering a sharp cry as he fell. He knew that Traill turned round at the sound and uttered an exclamation, he knew that he came towards him and picked him up, and so at last he stood there facing him, the two of them alone in a grey, empty world.

But Mr. Perrin was trembling so that he could not speak—trembling with cold, trembling with excitement, but trembling also with rage because Traill had found him in so ludicrous a position.

III

Traill's first exclamation had been one apparently of surprise at there being any one there at all; but now, as he stepped back and looked at the white, untidy figure before him—wild enough in that uncertain light—it seemed an exclamation of recognition and surprise, and a little of alarm.

'Why—Perrin!'

He had stepped back some steps away.

'Yes.' Perrin tried to pull himself together. He drew himself up and flung back his straggling hair. 'I am very wet—I am very cold.' His teeth chattered furiously. 'Why did you come out?' It was almost, in the way he said it, a pathetic appeal to him not to have come out—to have left things, if he could only have known, just as they were.

'I came,' Traill said as lightly as he could, although his voice was grave, 'because I couldn't sleep; you know, I've been overdone lately and sleeping badly.' Then he repeated almost sharply, 'I couldn't sleep, so I came out.'

'Yes—I saw you come out.'

'I know. I knew that you were following me.'

'You knew all the time?'

'Yes, I heard you coming downstairs. I wanted to know why you were following me.'

'Do you know now?'

'No.'

They stood in silence, facing one another. Traill had never lighted his pipe, but he was pulling at it furiously. His eyes never left Perrin's face.

'I followed you because I hate you—because I meant—I mean—to do for you.' Mr. Perrin's teeth were chattering with cold.

Traill did not seem disturbed at that; he shifted a little from one foot to the other, and then he went on gravely: 'Yes, I suppose I know that—really, I have known it a long time. I was awake when you came into my room the other night. I have been watching you. But what I do really want to know—what I've wanted to know all along—is your reason, or reasons. I suppose you ought to tell me.'

'No.' Mr. Perrin shook his head miserably. 'It's so cold—I'm so cold. Can't you hear my teeth? There's been too much hanging about—

we can't talk here. My mind 's made up.' He put his hand inside his pocket.

But Traill made no movement, although it might have been a revolver that he had there. 'Yes, I know it isn't quite the place for talking, but before you kill a fellow it is only decent to give your reasons. I know that you have disliked me ever since I 've been here. Of course *that 's* been obvious enough; but what I haven't been able to see is why you should hate me so and do for me as you say.' All this very gravely, and his eyes never left Perrin's face.

Perrin nodded his head very seriously. 'Yes, I suppose it 's only fair I should give you my reasons. It 's all plain enough, really.'

He knew now that if Traill moved away he would run after him and cut his throat, it would all be quite easy; but whilst he stood there, motionless, he could do nothing—and he shifted beneath his eyes.

'You see,' he said reflectively, almost as though he was speaking to himself, 'you 've taken everything that I had away from me. I suppose that 's what it is. I never had very much. . . . I was never very lucky. I always meant to do well. I had great ambitions when I was a boy; but there are people like that—because they have a habit or a manner or something, people don't like them—just some little thing. I always used to hope that people would like me, and I would have done anything for any one if it happened.

But they never *did* like me, because of my manner a very little thing. . . . And then I came to Moffatt's, you know, and I suppose Moffatt's has been too much for me—it often is too much for a man. I suppose I am beaten; but Moffatt's helps all your worst things, and it doesn't make it easier, living so close and everything, if you are naturally irritable.'

'Yes, I know,' said Traill, nodding his head.

'Well,' went on Mr. Perrin, apparently pleased that Traill understood, 'it was just like that—I had ideals, and I lost them all. Nobody cared whether I liked them or no, and then they began to laugh at me, and I knew I oughtn't to be laughed at, really—because I had always meant to do well. And things got worse. Twenty years of Moffatt's is a terrible time. I was always hoping, each term, that things would be better, but each term it was worse.'

'Yes,' said Traill again, 'I know.'

'Yes,' said Perrin, nodding his head, as though he were arguing it all out for his own satisfaction, 'and then you came, and soon you began to laugh at me like the rest. Then you were popular, and I hated that; you took the boys away from me.'

'No,' broke in Traill, 'I 'm sure——'

'Ah, but you did,' said Perrin, shaking his head gravely; 'and then there were little things—I was a much older man, and we quarrelled over that umbrella. I was angry because now they would laugh at me all the more.'

'I was very sorry about that,' said Traill, 'but it was all so silly.'

'Ah,' said Perrin, 'it is the silly things that matter at Moffatt's. And then you see,' he added quite simply, 'I loved Miss Desart.'

'My God!' cried Traill, 'I never suspected that.'

'I have loved her for a long time—I had begun to think that she loved me. It seemed as though it would be my last chance, and that she would take me away from here—this dreadful place; and then when you took her, it was my last hope, and so I began to hate you. I hated you more and more. It is the one thing that I think about—you see, it is my only thing in life now, and lately I have been muddled—these examinations—my headaches—I don't know. But I am no good in the world—nobody wants me . . . so I will kill you, because you have made life no good to me, and then I will kill myself.'

'I am sorry,' answered Traill gravely, 'I did not know that you loved Miss Desart. I have been very wrong about the whole thing; but I did try several times to be friends, and you would not let me. But I am very careless, I suppose, about people's feelings. Let us be friends now, and I will be better.'

'No,' Perrin answered, coming quite close to Traill. 'My mind was made up a long time ago—it is quite determined. I am going to kill you. Also, you see, it will mean that I'm quite useless—that I can't do anything at all—if I don't.'

And then suddenly he drew the knife from his pocket. Traill saw it, and, perhaps because it was so unexpected, he uttered a little cry and stepped backwards, and with that step he was over the edge of the cliff. He made one frantic attempt to catch at the earth, but the grass gave way in his hand, and in an instant he was gone.

Perrin, as he saw him disappear, saw also that the sun, heralded by bars and clouds of golden light, was rising above the sea.

IV

Perrin's first strained sensation as he stood peering into the mist and darkness was one of silence. There had been a sound of rending soil, a clatter of stones and falling turf, a wild scream, and then the steady plunge of the sea and the advancing colour that cut the mist.

His next feeling was that he had not touched him. 'I didn't push him—I didn't push him!' he repeated wildly over and over again to himself, his teeth chattering, his hair blowing. 'O God! I didn't push him!'

He was dreadfully cold, and he had the impulse to run eagerly, tumultuously, away from the spot, but still a dreadful curiosity held him there. The horizon was now breaking into gold. Little bits of pink cloud rose soaring, and lines of light, like fingers drawn lovingly over grey silk, passed, crossing and recrossing, over the sea.

Mr. Perrin stepped to the very edge and peered over. It was still very dark, but he could see enough in the faintly shining circle of the cove below to discover that it was not really very deep, that that was not really a great way down. There were great hollows of darkness, and then a little light, and then darkness again; but he fancied, as he peered, that he could make out something black and huddled against the white sand—something that even seemed, perhaps, to move a little.

Then suddenly the strain at which he had been living through all these days gave way with a snap, and he sat down suddenly there on the sand, in the mist and the growing light, and, with his fingers pressed tightly to his face, wept and wept.

'I didn't want him to be killed—I didn't want to kill him—I 've been mad—I don't know what I 've been thinking—I didn't want to kill him—the poor boy, the poor boy—I didn't want to kill him!'

He rocked in his distress, and then grew quiet, and at last with staring eyes sat there, facing the sea. Suddenly the sun burst its bands. The warm light streamed out, and, away over the sea and the hill, the mist went flying in tangled skeins, and clouds and blue stole softly, timidly, into the grey air and water. The warmth touched Mr. Perrin's cheek.

He stood up again and looked over, and now he

saw quite distinctly something huddled there. He saw also that the tide was coming in with great rapidity; already it had covered most of the sand, and was nearly touching the ground where Traill's body lay. What was to be done? If he ran to fetch someone, it would be long before they could get a boat and come round the cliff, and by that time the water would have caught the body and have dragged it out to sea. No, it would be too late to fetch any one. He wondered as he stood there, beating his hands and looking down, how he could ever have hated that quiet figure. That had all left him. If the boy were alive, something must be done to help him—something. He looked passionately up and down the long white road, but there was no sign as yet of any one. No, he must himself do something—it rested on him.

He glanced despairingly about and then down again. The very thought of climbing up and down a height had always been terrible to him—he got dizzy so easily; but now he saw that, if any one were to help Traill, to climb down was the only thing to be done. The cliff's side seemed very black and grim, and slanted sheer down, with no holds or crevices in the rock, but there were tufts of grass that jutted out here and there; perhaps these might help him.

He glanced again around him, but there was perfect silence. The blue had mounted through all the sky, and now shone above him gloriously.

Every object now was distinct around him. He took off his coat and flung it down over the cliff, on to the sand below—he had an idea that he might want it when he got down there. Then he rolled up his sleeves and looked at his arms, and thought how thin they were; his mouth was very set and determined. He looked down anxiously again, and fancied that now he saw Traill move a little. The sea moved so gently, so pleasantly, that it was impossible to think of it as something dangerous, evil, devouring.

He sat on the edge of the cliff; then he turned round, and, with his back to the sun, his hands gripping the cliff, let himself down: just below his feet was a strong ledge of grass, and he swung for an instant clutching this, his legs dangling. Then a sudden paralysis came over him; he could not move. He hung there, swaying, the great black face of the cliff against his eyes, space beneath him, blue sky and infinite distance above him, sickness and terror at his heart. He was crying, with little whimpering noises, 'O God! O God!' again and again.

For some time he found cracks for his feet, and soon he had gone, it seemed to him, a long way. Then he found an uneven surface with his foot, and then, lowering the other foot, another piece of grass. From this he lowered himself again, and was again hanging in air, only now, he thought, not so far above the sand—he could hear the licking whisper of the waves very plainly.

His foot swung about, searching for another resting-place; and then suddenly, with a sickening leaping of everything to his throat, with a wild cry, and a great swinging, like a censer, of brown earth and blue heaven above him, the grass gave way, and he fell.

He was stunned, and he lay sprawling with his hands out and his mouth full of sand. Then he pulled himself together; he was not really hurt—it had not been very far to fall—only his ankle hurt him rather. But he limped across to the place where Traill lay. He bent over him. Traill was lying on his face, so Perrin pulled very gently his shoulder down and rolled him over. His face was cut and bleeding and very white, and one leg was crumpled beneath him in a way that showed it was broken. Perrin opened his coat and waistcoat and undid his shirt; his heart was beating—very faintly—but Traill was alive. Then he scooped with his hands and brought some water and rubbed Traill's forehead; but he did not stir—he probably had concussion of the brain, Perrin thought. Then Perrin sat down on the sand with his back to the rock, and made Traill as comfortable as he could against him. He rested his poor, bleeding head on his chest, and took his hands and rubbed them, and then looked about him and wondered what was next to be done. The little cove was very quiet and still, but the sea was touching his feet—every moment it was rising higher—and only behind him was the black cliff, frowning, uncompromising. He did not know what was to be done. For a moment he did not want to think. He had never before, in all his life, known anything like this protecting feeling that crept about him like a burning flame. Although he knew that Traill was unconscious, he could not help fancying that he was leaning against him—that he had, a little of his own free will, come closer to him.

But something must be done—the sea was above his boots, always very softly advancing, then playfully drawing back again, and then coming the next time a little further still. Something must be done. He gathered Traill closer to him, and rubbed his hands more fiercely; if only he would come to his senses, or if someone would come! He saw at last a long ledge of rock, higher up, that would hold them both, and he hoped that they might, perhaps, escape the sea there. He climbed on hands and knees to the ledge, and then bent down and dragged Traill up. It was a very great exertion, and Traill was terribly heavy; but at last they were both up there, crowded together, Traill's body lying heavily against Perrin. But, even now, things were not really very greatly improved. The sea was breaking now against the rock; it seemed another creature from the sea that had kissed the shore so gently in the early morning—now it dashed against the cliff, every wave climbing higher, and already it had touched Perrin's boot. He could see the white line of surf round the cove, whereas it had seemed but an instant ago that there had been a yellow strip of shining sand.

He knew that they were not safe where they were, the tide must soon turn—above he could see grass and sea-anemones in ledges of the rock that marked the sea's limit, but the rock on which they were must soon be covered. He prayed desperately; he knelt on his knees, clasping his hands together, frantically clutching Traill's arm, and then stroking his hair, and then gazing distractedly about him in the hope that there would be some human being. But there was no one—there was nothing now save sea and rock. Then, as he glanced up at the black wall of cliff, he saw that there was another, still smaller ridge above their heads. On this some tufts of grass were growing, so that he knew that it was safe, but it was very thin and narrow. . . . It would not hold both of them.

But Traill must be saved. . . . At all costs Traill must be dragged up higher. He found that by standing on the ridge on which they already were, and holding Traill's body in his arms, he could just reach the rock. He took the limp body, and, with all his force raising it, he moved it along the higher ledge. The rock was so narrow that Traill's hands and legs hung over the ledge, but it was safe: nothing could touch him, and at last someone would surely come. Something must be done to attract notice; he took his handkerchief, and tied it round Traill's boot, so that it hung white against the black cliff. Of course it was only a chance, but he suddenly remembered that there was a man who sometimes came in a boat and bathed in that cove before breakfast. He had seen him there, and other people had often noticed—in another half-hour he would perhaps arrive.

Meanwhile for himself . . .

Suddenly he was very tired. He sank down on his rock, white, exhausted. The waves beat on every side of him, and sometimes they rose and covered him. In a very little time it would be too late. He was already very wet. He looked once more up the side of the cliff. It rose sheer, black, uncompromising — there were no more clefts or holes, there was no hope for any foothold —besides, he was so weak now—he was trembling all over. . . . It had been very exhausting.

He sat and thought about it, and then suddenly, with the streaming sun, with the burning blue, with the white spray, he knew. It had come! It had come! He could shout it aloud to the world. It had come at last. . . . His chance!

He sat there, with his elbows on his knees, his face resting on his hands, looking out to sea. And so things had come to this at last! Although no one knew, although there was only about him that tossing sea, above him the sky, at his back the rock, at last he could be of use. The clown had his serious side, the walker-on in the pageant had his work, his great work to do. He smiled and then stood up, because the water now covered the face of his rock and was up to his knees; he had to stand with his back to the rock, because the waves when they rose buffeted his face.

He thought of the term—of the way that he had bullied boys, of the way that he had loved Miss Desart, of the way that he had hated Traill, of the meannesses and spite and petty anger. Was every one made of so many different people, had every one such base things, such miserably little things, to account for?

But now at last he was justified. No one would ever know—Traill would never know. . . .

Was it, he wondered, odd that he, who had intended during all these weeks to kill Traill, should now be giving his life for him? No . . . it was not really odd. One was as certain a justification as the other. And he thought of it now as a curious fact that the nearer the time for killing Traill had come, the less he had hated him. He was not a big enough character to kill any one. . . . It was much easier to die for someone. All that he had ever needed in life was a justification—a reason why he, Vincent Perrin, should exist at all—and it was because Moffatt's had robbed him of that justification that he had hated it so. Now he was justified.

The waves struck his face—one had almost dragged him off his feet. 'It 's a good thing,' he said, 'that that fellow bathes here in the morning. He 'll see that handkerchief . . . the old lady will have my £100. . . .' And then, after a pause, 'Miss Desart will never know.'

He took Traill's hand which hung down, and very lightly kissed it. He would not wait any more—there was nothing more to be done.

He took his last look at the sea and the sky, and he laughed once because he had never been so happy in his life before, and then he let himself go. The sea, leaping, tossing, tumbling about the rock, covered the place where he had been.

CHAPTER XV

PERRIN REQUIESCAT

I

Breakfast that morning at the Combers' was a very cheerful meal. It was half-past eight, the day was brilliantly fine, and nearly all the boys had gone. The earlier their departure the better they were pleased, and most of them had caught the eight o'clock train.

Now there was a strange, wonderful peace—suddenly the tension was relaxed, and for a time, for a short time, Moffatt's was not a school but a home.

The Marmadukery that had reigned so triumphantly on the preceding day had disappeared as quickly as it had come. Sir Marmaduke had been hustled back into his grave again, and only in the scattered flower-pots that had decorated the school hall, and in the chairs that were piled on top of one another in the passages outside, could any signs of him be seen.

But in the Comber dining-room all thoughts of him were very far away. The sun streamed through the windows and fell on the sausages and the coffee and the marmalade and all the things that the sun ought to fall on at an English breakfast-table in the morning. It also fell on Mrs. Comber, who was trying to give orders to Jane, the housemaid, attend to Freddie, and smile at Isabel, all at the same time; it also fell on Mr. Comber, who had put on a Norfolk jacket and knickerbockers as a sign that term was really over, and on Isabel.

'No, Jane, I did *not* say, "Get the quilts out of the store-cupboard," because you know perfectly well that most of the quilts are out already, and—Have another sausage, Freddie; there are plenty here, and they are so good this morning. I have never eaten better anywhere, and it is all because I went to Harrison this time, instead of Quern's, although he is just a tiny bit more expensive; but it 's really worth it, if you know what you 're getting, and aren't afraid of being put off with all sorts of shams, and of course you never know with a sausage—No, Jane, I really can't attend to you now: come to me afterwards, and I 'll tell you what I mean. Isabel, my dear, you haven't got any coffee—you must have some more—I insist.'

Mrs. Comber was outrageously happy. Mr. Comber had only the evening before received the offer of a post at the Kensington Museum which would suit him exactly, and the salary attached to it, although nothing very tremendous, made the acceptance of the post comfortable. For years Mrs. Comber had expected such a letter.

At one time it had seemed that it must come, that it was merely a question of waiting. Then gradually hope had died. Freddie was too old—men did not get posts at his age—and then suddenly, through the urgency of an old friend, this piece of work had been found for him.

Escape at last, and just when she had given up all hope! 'My dear,' she said, when she was telling Isabel about it, 'you could have done anything you liked to me when I heard about it, and I shouldn't have known. I cried, and then I kissed Freddie, and then I cried again. Oh, my dear, such a mess, and it isn't right we should all be so happy!'

But they were all just as happy as they could be, and Freddie himself seemed to change, to brighten, to broaden, under the influence of his approaching escape.

When breakfast was over, Mrs. Comber and Isabel stood at the window, their arms linked, looking out on to the grass that shone and glittered beneath the sun.

'I suppose,' said Mrs. Comber, 'that, although I 've hated the place so much and so long, and wanted, God knows, with all my heart and soul to get away from it, I have never, until now, realized the wickedness of it. When I think of what this term has been, of the way we all felt, of the things we might have done——'

'Yes,' said Isabel, very gravely, 'it was having a dreadful effect on Archie. I have never seen any one change so quickly. His nerves seemed to be going all to bits. I am most tremendously glad we are going. I wish with all my heart that every one else was going too. Places like this oughtn't to be allowed to continue another week.'

'Where is your Archie?' said Mrs. Comber.

'Oh, he will be over here in a minute. I expect that he will sleep late this morning after so many mornings of getting up at half-past six. By the way, what 's poor little Garden Minimus doing wandering round in that disconsolate way?'

'Oh, he doesn't leave until to-night; his brothers are going to London, but he is crossing over to Ireland. Yes, he looks rather disconsolate. Yes, dear, now that we are going to London too, I am tremendously glad that you are both leaving here. It would never have done for Archie, although of course he had a bad start, fighting Mr. Perrin like that.'

'Poor Mr. Perrin!' Isabel sighed. She still saw him as he had been on that day when he congratulated her on her engagement. She felt in some secret, undefined way that she was responsible, a little, for his unhappiness. 'Poor Mr. Perrin!'

'Well, I don't know,' said Mrs. Comber, 'now that we 're going, I suppose it is fair enough to say that I never liked Mr. Perrin—in fact, I disliked him very much. I am sure I don't know what those kind of people are for, with all their stiff, awkward manners, and their selfishness, and their difficulties. People say, "Oh, it 's nerves," and then think they have excused a man, but I think it 's downright selfishness. Now, you never can imagine Mr. Perrin doing anything for anybody, or thinking about anything in the world except his own silly squabbles. He 's a nasty, selfish, ill-tempered man, and I 'm glad I 'm not going to see any more of him.'

'That 's unlike you,' Isabel said; 'you aren't generally unkind about people.'

'Well, his making such a fuss about his silly umbrella annoyed me. He 's a selfish, horrid creature.'

'But we all made a fuss,' said Isabel.

'We wouldn't have if he hadn't,' said Mrs. Comber triumphantly. But in any case Isabel was bound to feel that Mr. Perrin didn't matter very much, and that, in a way, was tragedy sufficient. He was a part of Moffatt's, as the ink-stained benches and the long stone corridors were part of it. Now they were leaving Moffatt's and all that belonged to it, and they would never think of it or of Mr. Perrin again. As she moved back from the window, humming a little tune, she dismissed Mr. Perrin for ever.

As she turned her back and moved down the room, she was conscious suddenly of steps, many steps, on the gravel outside; but there were no voices, only the tread of feet.

She turned back to the window; but before she reached it, the door was opened sharply, and Mrs. Comber stood there, her face very white, her hands outstretched. Behind her, as in a mist, there were other faces.

Isabel knew. Her lips moved, and she gasped, 'Archie!' Then, with a supreme effort, she pulled herself together, and stood very straight and still, whilst Mrs. Comber came forward.

Then she said, very quietly, 'Tell me—is he dead?'

'No, dear.' Mrs. Comber eagerly took her hands. 'He has had a bad fall from the cliff; he is unconscious, concussion, and his leg is broken. The doctor is there, there is no——'

Isabel went, very straight, with her head up, out of the room, upstairs, to the little white-boarded chamber where they had laid him.

The doctor was there; the window was open, and the sun streamed in across the blue carpet, and with its light came the scent of the trees and the cold, sharp air of the winter morning. She was on her knees by his bedside and had taken his white hand in hers.

In the afternoon he came to himself, and knew her and held her hand very tightly. But in that long vigil that she had by the side of his bed, she had, suddenly, become a woman. In the stress of the instant, in the summoning of all her forces to her aid, she had flung aside once and for all the inexperience, the hesitations, of growing up. Life had become a battle—it had before been a game—but now the prize was greater. . . .

II

Garden Minimus had to wait for the evening train. He cursed his fate, but no amount of cursing altered the fact that he had to put in a day with nothing very especial to do and no one very especial to talk to. There were one or two other unfortunates in the same case as himself, but they were none of them people with whom he had anything in common: Thompson Major was too lofty, being in the Sixth, and having his colours for cricket; Crebbett Minor was too lowly, being in the First, and having nothing at all except a stammer and a spotty complexion.

Moreover, there was something that Garden wanted to do—he wanted to speak to Mr. Perrin. He had wanted to speak to him for a great many days, but he had put it off from hour to hour because 'a chap felt such an awful fool saying he was sorry and all that kind of rot.' But he *was* sorry, tremendously sorry. Perrin had been most awfully kind to him for terms and terms, but this time Garden's back had been up: he'd behaved like a most awful rotter, and he would have liked to put Perrin's mind all right about things before the holidays came. He had intended to speak to him last night at the concert, but Perrin had not been at the concert. He got up very early to share in the jubilations of his departing friends, and then, after they had gone, he wandered about, and nearly plucked up courage to knock on Perrin's bedroom door.

He could not find Perrin—he asked people, but they were all very busy: 'Mr. Perrin had not got up yet.'

Garden felt very unhappy. Everything was so empty now that every one had gone; the spirit of desolation was abroad. Life was a thing of littering paper, of gaping forms, of dusty floors. He went down to the cliffs, and here the splendour of the day cheered him. It was amazingly warm for December. The sea in the cove sparkled and glittered, and even the black rock seemed to smile.

He stood above the cove and looked out to sea. . . .

Perrin, although he was a bit of an ass, was really a good sort. . . . He would behave more decently next term. He would make up a bit. . . . He was a queer beggar, Perrin, but he meant to be decent to him . . . next term.

His tiny figure made a black dot against the shining surface of the long, white road.